STARGAZERS

LP HERNANDEZ

CEMETERY GATES
MEDIA

Stargazers
Published by Cemetery Gates Media
Binghamton, New York

Copyright © 2022
by LP Hernandez

All rights reserved. Without limiting the rights under the copyright reserved above, no part of this publication may be reproduced, stored in, or introduced into a retrieval system, or transmitted in any form or by any means (electronic, mechanical, photocopying, recording, or otherwise) without prior written permission.

ISBN: 9798800752939

My Dark Library #1

For more information about this book and other Cemetery Gates Media publications, visit us at:

cemeterygatesmedia.com
twitter.com/cemeterygatesm
instagram.com/cemeterygatesm

Cover Artist and Design: Carrion House

Title page illustration by Ryan Mills

For Maggie. I loved you before I knew you.

FOREWORD

This is the first novella in a series called **My Dark Library** that I curated in partnership with Cemetery Gates Media. So this foreword is a little extra special and I hope it will set the tone for the series. I want this to be me, "Mother Horror", talking to you.

Reader to reader.

Nothing fussy or flowery, just my lips to your ears talking about this author who wrote this book and why I chose it for you. For me. For My Dark Library. LP Hernandez wasn't someone I knew about until suddenly, he was. That's not to say he wasn't out there doing his thing. He's popular over at *The No Sleep Podcast* with a lot of stories on their platform you can listen to and enjoy. I just wasn't aware of *The No Sleep Podcast* until recently.

LP(Les) answered a call at Cemetery Gates and when it was accepted, there was a tweet that caught my eye. Joe (EIC at Cemetery Gates) tweeted, "This story's so wild that LP tried to withdraw it while we were reading it. 'Cemetery Joe' isn't the original title of the story, either. Had to request a title change so we could print it."

I noticed.

Fast forward a few weeks and Ashley Sawyers and I open the submissions call for our *Human Monsters* anthology with Dark Matter Magazine and one day, a story from LP Hernandez shows up called, "The Bystander".

I jump right into it because I've seen this name, right? I remembered what Joe tweeted.

Holy hell. "The Bystander" blew our minds! Wait until you read it.

I simultaneously have this My Dark Library submission call going so I send a message to Les nudging him to submit a story. I wanted to see what else this guy could do! He responds that he was right in the middle of writing a novella titled *Stargazers* for my call. I was so excited! My thought was if he could stick the landing with horror in short fiction, what're a few more thousand words to get a novella out there? I had high hopes.

Obviously, since you're holding *Stargazers* in your hands now, LP Hernandez more than met expectations. People know I'm all about that horror with heart. Horror lands its punches when readers are invested in the fictional lives of characters they have developed feelings for. Such is the case with *Stargazers*. A worldwide, catastrophic event that is impacting the lives of so many people, but Hernandez zeroes in on just a few. One family. Their personal struggle to survive. Readers will watch a father fight to protect his daughter no matter the cost. This is a story about love, loss, and hope for a life worth living. I hope you enjoy it. Keep an eye on LP Hernandez! He's doing great things.

    Sadie Hartmann
    April 22, 2022

First recorded documentation of the Stargazers phenomenon.

"My Neighbor Has Been Staring at the Moon for Hours"

29 January 2023, 2:32 PM - User **Anon11209102**:

Breaking the fourth wall a bit here. I know this forum is for supposedly true scary stories that more than likely are not true. I've been a lurker for a few years, never thought I would have a reason to post. I'm not very creative with my words so you'll have to forgive if I just lay it out there as it happened. I'll try to make it interesting.

First, I live in a hybrid rural-suburb. Each house has about an acre of land around it with quite a few trees between properties and some pockets of forest here and there. A good place for amateur astronomy most nights. My husband and I bought a telescope with our tax return this year, though I use it more than him because he can't stand the mosquitoes.

It wasn't a great night for the telescope. The clouds were sporadic enough I hadn't caught sight of anything clearly for more than a minute at a time.

A little before midnight I gave up. I put the protective drape over the telescope and noticed my neighbor, a retiree I'll call Doug, standing on his deck. There was a bit of moon-glow, but the clouds absorbed most of the light. I couldn't see him clearly, just the shape of him against the backdrop of the deck. I almost called out but didn't. It was so quiet. It felt like I was spying on him. Instead, I just watched.

My eyes adjusted to the low light, enough that I was certain it was Doug and not a deck chair with a hat on it or something. But I couldn't understand what he was doing. He just stood there with his head back, looking at the sky. His arms were limp by his sides. He didn't sway, scratch himself, swat at a mosquito. I mean, it is winter but the bugs don't seem to know it down here in the South.

As one minute stretched into three I began to doubt that it was Doug. He's in his mid-sixties, I think. Not brittle but not in the best shape. He's in the "riding lawnmower" years now, usually sipping a Coors Light. After ten minutes I had to sit when my lower back started barking at me. Fifteen minutes. Twenty.

It had to be Doug. The silhouette didn't make sense otherwise. Even from one hundred feet away I could spot the swell of his belly. I checked on my husband, asleep. Considered waking him but didn't. I swapped my slippers for sneakers and exited the backyard through the side gate.

*Doug was just standing on his deck, staring at the night sky. Up close a few details revealed themselves, but I didn't gain any new information. I only knew it was Doug and not some weird, scarecrow version of him because I could see his chest rise and fall, just slightly. I imagined him turning to his left and noticing me, standing in **his** yard in my bathrobe and tennis shoes.*

I returned to my house, slid into bed without waking my husband, but I couldn't sleep. Every half hour or so I would wriggle out of the blankets and peer through the blinds. Every half hour Doug was standing on his deck, staring at the sky. For hours and hours this went on. Finally, at dawn, he was gone.

There's no twist. I don't have an explanation. Has this happened to anyone else? I told my husband about it and he nodded, said "that's strange" a dozen times as he dressed for work.

I didn't think he understood a word I said or actually believed it was strange. But he called me on the way to work and said Doug was walking on the side of the road heading out of town.

"Kinda strange," he said.

My husband, the wordsmith.

Thanks for reading. If anyone's ever heard of anything like this feel free to DM me.

29 January 2023, 4:12 PM - User **Danightstalka595:**

Wish I could get the five minutes it took me to read this back. Not scary.

29 January 2023, 4:38 PM – User **Banana$tand24:**

Did you try turning him off and on again?

CHAPTER ONE - BLIND

The cell phone chime could have been a raptor screech for the effect it had on the room, a dozen pairs of white or silver eyebrows arching over disapproving gazes. Eyes held together by webs of pulsing capillaries peered over the frames of bifocals and color-change lenses that rarely saw the sun. Judith patted her pants pocket, thumb searching for the button that would prevent additional interruptions. It was Henry, of course. It was always Henry. She knew without checking.

"Sorry," she said, the dongle held like a grenade against her chest. "Where was I?"

She turned her attention to the bar graph of statistics about slips, trips, and falls within the hospital system projected on the screen behind her. The administrator at the head of the table sighed so forcefully a smattering of raspy chuckles followed.

"Mrs. Silva, you were talking about an initiative to post additional signage around the water dispensers. Did you *touch base* with the facility manager or is this the first forum you have presented this plan?"

She smiled, reading between the lines of the corporate language. She *had* met with the facility manager. *That* information was presented on the previous slide, which suggested the administrator had not paid attention to it. Before she could reply, her cell phone chimed again, louder this time. Instead of muting the phone she increased its volume.

She fished the phone out of her pocket, cheeks hot as a sunburn.

"Sorry. My, uh, husband probably can't find the remote," Judith said.

She pressed the home button, intending to power off the device. A message preview caught her eye for a half a second as the screen went black.

NEWS!! NOW!!!

"That should do it," she said, returning the lifeless device to her pocket.

The graph was meaningless, numbers blurring out of focus. The starch of the medical director's lab coat tickled her nostrils, the urge to sneeze watering her eyes.

DUNNA DUNNA DUNNA DUNNA DUNNA DUNNA DUNNA DUNNA.

The administrator silenced his phone.

"Was that *Batman*, Carl?" the Chief Financial Officer asked.

BLIP

The man plucked his own cell phone from his pocket and frowned at the screen.

Within seconds, the table was a kicked hornet's nest of buzzing cell phones. Bifocals were adjusted on noses or retrieved from shirt pockets.

Chapped lips mumbled words as though to speak above a whisper would make them come true. The administrator looked up from his phone, spotted Judith in front of the screen displaying the meaningless bar graph. He chewed his lip and loosened his tie as the other executives volleyed strange looks around the table. She flashed back to September of 2001. A senior in high school, she recalled the impromptu march to the gymnasium where the principal struggled to explain something she did not understand.

Judith powered on the cell phone.

"Mrs. -uh- Sylva?" the administrator said. He placed the phone screen-down on the table, knuckled it a few inches away.

"Yes?"

Her cell phone found a signal and the missed messages pinged across the screen.

"Does that connect to cable?"

She followed the direction of his pointing finger.

"The projector? No. It connects to the computer. I can pull something up online if you need."

Fourteen messages and six missed phone calls.

ITS HAPPENING AGAIN

"Would you mind pulling up a news site? Should be on any."

The gentleness of his tone was uncharacteristic.

"Um, sure," Judith said, leaving the dongle on the table and sliding behind the lectern.

She minimized the safety presentation and clicked on a browser. There was no need to search for a news site. The browser's home page was dominated by one story.

USS GERALD R. FORD SUNK

Cell phones were pocketed in favor of a live video of the aircraft carrier half-submerged in the waters off the coast of Virginia. Of the whispered words exchanged around the table, one was uttered with increasing frequency, *how?*

Lacking information as to the reason for the sinking, the reporter regurgitated facts about its size, the make-up of its crew. How had the ship sunk? The answer to that question presented very different possibilities about the future of the world. Judith gripped the lectern to keep from falling.

I can't go back Judy. I can't go back.

She swiped the screen and typed. *It's okay. Sure it's an accident. They can't make you go back.*

"Mrs. Sylva, we're going to have to reschedule this briefing," the administrator said, then sighed and removed his glasses to rub his eyes. "Thank you for putting patient safety first."

"Yes sir," Judith said as she scrolled through the missed messages.

"What are those?" a doctor nearby said.

Judith squinted at the projection on the screen. There was movement on the deck of the sinking ship, slow, almost too slow to catch the eye.

"It's the crew," she said. "They're in a line, walking. They're jumping off the ship one-by-one."

"It's not on fire. Or at least not on the deck. Why would they do that?" the doctor asked, blinking at Judith as if she truly knew the answer.

"I don't know. I remember the jumpers on 9-11, but this…" she trailed off, shook her head and cradled herself.

Her cell phone chimed again.

It wasn't an accident.

***

Henry's fingers flexed open and closed as if attempting to stimulate two dead hearts back to life. There was a lightness in his chest, a sensation of some vital part of him pulling away leaving a bumbling avatar behind. He stared at the television without blinking, eyes tracing letters to words he could not assemble. The tissue of his lungs became gauze, unable to contain the trembling breaths.

Penny fumbled with the straps of her apron. Her attention shifted between her daddy, whose lips were moving without sound, and the plastic food in the skillet of her play kitchen. Could plastic food burn if not properly tended? She did not know, and maybe her daddy wouldn't notice when she served it to him. At the very least she hoped the meal would distract him from whatever had stolen the words from his mouth. She turned the burner knob a few times just to be sure.

Henry glanced at his phone. Accident? An aircraft carrier sinking was not an accident, not something that happened because someone forgot to flip a switch. Though he did not serve in the Navy he understood the act was sabotage on a scale not seen since Pearl Harbor. The coordination to access the carrier…it was a conspiracy, and not in the JFK sense of the word. It was the conspiring of probably dozens of individuals.

"Daddy?"

"Hmm?" he said, speaking through his avatar.

"Are those ants on the boat?" Penny stirred the plastic squash, dusted an empty pepper shaker over it. "They look like ants, the sidewalk ants. How they walk in a line like remember when I dropped my ice-cream outside?"

"Yeah, Penny."

"Are they lining up for ice-cream, Daddy?"

She tried to flip the plastic food like the cooking shows her father watched, but the veggies jumped out the skillet and landed on the floor. She retrieved them, bare fingered, making little hiss noises as if plastic was actually hot.

"I don't think so."

"What are they doin'?"

Henry blinked, found his daughter's face, then returned his attention to the screen. He had not sat since the news broke, instead found a dozen ways to lean against the living room wall. Behind the ship was a blue infinity, little waves tipped with sunlight. Every few seconds the waves were disrupted by the ripples and froth of a body breaking upon the water as another sailor lept to his death.

There was no panic, no desperate thrashing of arms. This was not an escape. It was part of it, the jumpers.

"Daddy?"

Penny arranged the food on a plate. She could *almost* smell it. Unlike real food, though, her creation slid back and forth with each step, coaxing the bubble gum tip of her tongue to part her lips.

"Yes?"

After several seconds of stock footage of the carrier, the live shot briefly zoomed on the line of men and women inching toward the precipice. Sailors, all, but they were not uniform in appearance. Some wore blue, utility coveralls, while others were dressed for bed, sweatpants and t-shirts. Henry scratched behind his ear, lungs straining to take flight as he noticed at least a few of the Sailors were not wearing pants.

"What are they doin'?" Penny tried again.

He felt a nudge above his knee. His daughter hoisted the plate of plastic food. Henry took it, an ear of corn slipping off as he did.

"Oh, that's okay!" Penny said, blowing lint off the corn and passing it to her father.

"Thank you."

The static encroaching upon the borders of his vision retreated as he focused on Penny's hopeful smile, eyes like caramel gum drops. The voice from the TV, which left no space between words for a single breath, faded into a drone, like the hum of the highway beneath rolling tires.

"Careful!" Penny said as her father pinched a plastic chicken thigh.

Henry understood and blew on the toy, prompting a nod from his daughter. He touched the plastic with his lips and made exaggerated *nom nom* chewing sounds. Penny crossed her arms over her chest, ear slightly cocked to receive his praise.

"Ran out of salt," she sighed.

They were always going on about salt on the cooking shows, salt and something called *acid*. Penny didn't know what the word meant, but the thought of it conjured lemons in her mind.

"It's perfect," Henry said.

Penny nodded.

"Oh, do you have a fork?" Henry asked.

Penny smacked her forehead and dashed to the play kitchen. She rummaged through the dishes in the strainer and returned with a sea green fork.

"Thank you," Henry said, and tapped the tines against the glossy surface of the mashed potatoes.

"They're really good together," Penny offered.

"Oh, right."

Henry alternated between plastic chicken and plastic mashed potatoes. He pursed his lips while chewing nothing, as if giving genuine consideration to the flavor of the combined foods.

"Better than perfect!" he announced.

Penny understood her daddy didn't actually consume the food but hadn't rectified that knowledge with the feedback he offered.

"Not too much acid?" she asked, testing how the word felt in her mouth.

"Just the right amount," Henry said. "Here, let me help with the dishes."

Penny mimed wiping sweat from her brow.

"Can I put on my show?" she asked.

Henry glanced at the TV. Stock footage again, text in three different places on the screen. Just before the wings in his lungs could flutter to life the image vanished and a cartoon tiger wearing a red sweater appeared.

Penny watched her father from the corner of her eye. He held a skillet under the faucet and made a *ksshhhh* sound to replicate water flowing. She sighed, smiled, and turned back to the television.

***

Henry did not respond to Judith's message. He sent no new updates over lunch. She sat at her desk, statistics in a font too small to read on one screen and breaking news on the other. By the absence of overhead pages, she suspected most employees were similarly non-productive, and so she left early. As much as she tried to justify her position and salary, she wasn't actively saving lives, and the unanswered text might as well have been a siren complete with flashing lights.

Judith drove home with the radio volume low. As with the hallways in the hospital, the roads felt abandoned, a few cars driving at or under the speed limit instead of ten miles over it. The sinking of the Gerald Ford would have dominated news cycles for weeks, but the strange circumstances surrounding it set the world on a knife's edge, quivering in the wind. She turned the radio volume up.

"...second American aircraft carrier to sink along with a Chinese carrier. Both governments have yet to offer

17

explanations for the incidents. Reports are now coming in from around the world about…"

Judith muted the radio. The steering wheel was slick with sweat. She hummed to drown out the thoughts coalescing in her mind. Three aircraft carriers sunk in one day. Reports of…well, she didn't know. She wouldn't allow herself to think about it just yet.

What was Henry thinking? She made the immediate connection to 9/11 and was certain he'd done the same. The day changed little for her beyond the way it impacted every American. For Henry, just a teenager that day, it was a domino that would lead him to the other side of the world nearly a decade later. The man who returned to her was not the same man who left.

She pulled into the driveway having no recollection of the previous twenty minutes of her drive. There was a Christmas wreath on the door, still. The holiday was over a month ago, but Henry didn't notice things like that. Which version of him waited beyond the door?

"I'm home!" Judith announced, kicking off her heels as she crossed the threshold into the house.

"Mommy!" Penny shrieked down the hallway, leaping into Judith's arms.

"Hey, sweetie! How was your day?"

"Good! I made lunch for Daddy and then we watched *my* shows and took a nap together. We made food too! It's not ready, Mommy! You're not s'posed to be home yet!"

"Oh, well, they said I could go home early. Where's Dad?"

"He's in the kitchen," Penny wriggled free, coming halfway out of her nightgown. "Daddy! Mommy's here! You gotta get the plates!"

Which version of Henry was this? He glanced over his shoulder as she entered the kitchen, smiled; but his attention was on the steaming pot in front of him.

"Hey babe," he said.

"Hey, how's things?"

"Oh, good enough I guess. You're early?"

She unbuttoned her blazer, "Yeah, there wasn't much going on at work. I was in a meeting when the first carrier sank."

His shoulders flinched. The wooden spatula slipped from his fingers and boiling water splashed out of the pot.

"The *first?*"

Judith swallowed, "Yeah, weren't you watching? I figured that's why you stopped texting. It's been on the news all day."

Henry abandoned his post at the stove, zombie-walked to the living room. The tiger with the red sweater waved as if anticipating his dismissal, and the next image was of the President of the United States speaking in the Oval Office. Henry sat on the edge of the couch, chin cupped in one hand, the other frozen in mid-air with the remote aimed at the television.

Penny tugged her mother's sleeve. Her eyebrows strained to unite above the bridge of her scrunched nose, and she perched her hands on her hips the same way Judith did just before a lecture.

She whispered-shouted, "It was making Daddy sad, so I changed the channel!"

Judith nodded, glanced from the steaming pot back to her husband. His chest rose and fell in little bursts, barely controlled. She padded into the living room.

"Babe…it…it doesn't mean anything for you. They can't make you go back in. Not with the way you left."

Henry didn't blink.

He was somewhere else now.

The remote slipped from his hand. Penny retrieved it, offered it to him, but her daddy wasn't there. He was in that other place he sometimes went to, somewhere inside of himself.

30 January 2023, 11:45 AM User – **Ruffntumble0854:**

OP, the same thing happened to me. I've been going crazy the last few hours, finally sat down and started scrolling just to take my mind off things and found your post. I don't know what's going on, but it happened to my husband. I went to bed early last night, challenging day with the kids and I just needed the extra sleep. Hubby usually comes to bed around midnight. Actually, he usually falls asleep on the couch and wakes up around midnight then stumbles to bed.

It was after midnight when I woke. I didn't check the time then, but I did after. Hubby wasn't in bed, and I didn't see the light from the TV under the bedroom door. Went to the bathroom and then to the living room to check on him. It was dark, just the light above the stove I left on a few hours ago.

I crept upstairs, checked the kids' rooms. Sometimes they have bad dreams and he lays with them. Both asleep and no sign of hubby. At this point I was more confused than afraid. Our office is a work in progress, transitioning from a spare bedroom, but I checked anyway. Not there.

It didn't make sense he would drive anywhere. He would have woken me up. His keys were hanging where they always are. Still, I checked the driveway simply because there was nowhere else.

I screamed when I opened the front door and found him there. He was standing just like your neighbor, OP. Head turned to the sky, mouth open. I didn't know what to think in the moment. I've never experienced anything like it before. Was he sleepwalking? It was the only thing that made sense then, and it didn't really make sense.

You're not supposed to wake sleepwalkers, right? I didn't know if that was a real thing or one of those 'facts' everyone knows which is not true, like bubblegum staying in your stomach for seven years.

It's winter and I live up north. Hubby was wearing his comfy clothes, a long-sleeve shirt and flannel pajama bottoms. Cozy for inside but not enough for twenty degrees. He was barefoot, skin touching concrete that was cold enough to freeze water. I called his name. I nudged him. I shook him.

It was like trying to move a mountain.

He wouldn't budge. Didn't react. I tried for an hour. By two o'clock I gave up. I put his winter coat on him as best I could. I wrapped a blanket around his shoulders and piled towels around his feet.

Maybe I should have done more. I don't know. I ran out of ideas. I moved to the couch, watched TV, checked on him every fifteen minutes. I threw the towels in the dryer so they were at least warm.

Hubby is gone.

It was around 5 AM. Went to replace the towels and he was not there. I walked outside, called his name. Nothing. I ran to the sidewalk and thought I saw him walking toward me. I took three steps toward him before I realized it was someone else. Someone not quite dressed for the weather. He walked past me as if I wasn't there. I turned to watch him walk and saw two others just the same as him. Women, I think. One wore only an oversized t-shirt and one slipper.

I don't know where they were headed, but they were all going the same direction.

Hubby has not come back. I've made all the phone calls. I've driven over one-hundred miles just doing laps around town.

OP, if you figure anything out please DM me. To the trolls on this thread…something is happening. Just pray it doesn't happen to you.

30 January 2023, 12:17 PM - User **Danightstalka595:**

So…OP made another account bc the first story bombed? How about learn to write instead of resorting to gimmicks.

30 January 2023, 1:14 PM – User **Fears4tears_23:**

My mom is gone. I don't know what's going on…there's a lot of scary shit happening right now. The front door was open when I woke up.

30 January 2023, 1:28 PM – User **TruckinwithJeezus:**

I drive overnight. Mostly short routes. Three hours there, three hours back. Pulled into my neighborhood around five this AM and passed at least a dozen people walking, mostly wearing night clothes. It's cool here, but not cold.

My daughter is gone. Wife thinks she ran away because she's done it before. The front door was open. Nothing's missing from her room. I hope she ran away. I hope she wasn't one of the people I passed early in the morning not even realizing it was her.

Stay safe OP. I think you're right. Something is happening.

CHAPTER TWO - SIMMER

They agreed to leave the television on during dinner, with the caveat it would be muted with subtitles. Henry stirred food on his plate while seldom looking at it, the spaghetti noodles crackling like plastic wrapping. Penny, from her booster seat, glared at her mother.

"What is it?"

Penny's face pinched into a mask of anger. She chewed aggressively, red sauce slapping her cheeks as she inhaled the pasta.

"Penny?"

The girl glanced at her father, noodles trembling on the tips of the tines like worms plucked from darkness of the earth and thrust into sunlight.

"Daddy was okay," she said.

Judith blinked, lips parting to reveal a bite half-chewed.

"I helped him feel better. Now he feels bad again."

Judith shook her head. *She* was to blame? Henry was going to find out. It was a worldwide event. Rebuttals gathered in her mind, adult logic with words the child would not understand threatening to burst through the dam of her clenched teeth.

Henry was unaware of the storm brewing only feet from him. He held his fork below his chin not realizing all the noodles had slipped free. His lips moved as he read the subtitles and his free hand probed his body, traced the shiny scars hidden beneath his shirt.

This would not be good for them, Judith accepted. Whatever it was and however long it took, it would not be good for them. She saw in Henry a man she loved, still. But there were times she wondered if he was **the** man she loved, if there could never be another. This Henry was a combination of *her* Henry and something else, something like a cat gone feral, one that could not distinguish friend from predator.

"I'm sorry," Judith said in a voice far from apologetic.

"He was okay," Penny said.

"He'll be okay," Judith said, pairing the lies together. "There's some things going on in the world and Daddy just needs some time to process it—I mean, to understand it."

Penny glanced over her shoulder. There were six people on the screen in different boxes. Only one was speaking. What did he need to understand about that?

She tried to hold onto her anger. She didn't like the way her daddy forgot how to smile, forgot to say nice words to her. But there was a lot she wanted to tell her mother. There was cookie dough in the refrigerator and Penny helped make it. Also, she learned a new song about numbers. She couldn't be mad at Mommy and also tell her everything about her day.

Penny sighed, "It's okay. Just don't do it again, please."

Judith allowed the follow-up question to die on her tongue. Instead, she nodded and reached across the table to wipe pasta sauce from her daughter's cheek.

***

"Your breath smells like cookies," Judith said.

Penny covered her mouth and giggled through her fingers, "Oops! Daddy usually brushes my teeth, but he was gone."

Judith nodded, "Yeah, this is the understanding part I was talking about. Daddy just needs some time. We'll get those sugar bugs on your teeth in the morning, okay?"

She wasn't convinced Henry only needed time. It was a mantra she repeated to convince herself to start a family. He deserved it, for the man he was if not for the man he became.

"Why are you crying, Mommy?"

Judith wiped her eye, "Am I? Sorry, just extra tired tonight. I had a big meeting at work that kind of ended before it started. Just felt...unfinished I guess."

They watched the winking stars of Penny's projector nightlight orbit the smoke detector. Penny talked about how the constellations got their names, knowledge she gained from her father, until her words became shapeless, melting into raspy breaths. Judith pinched herself to stay awake. To attempt to leave before her daughter was fully asleep was a mistake she had made many times in the past, and it often resulted in a second wind for Penny that would have them up until midnight.

On the cusp of sleep, Judith blinked awake. There was a new smell in the house, one that overtook the buttery-sweet scent of cookies. She wrinkled her nose and wriggled free of the comforter. Penny was fast asleep facing away from her. The door squeaked open, and she waited, halfway out of the room, for the sound of mattress springs shifting as Penny realized her mother was leaving. No sound but her daughter's breaths, and so Judith closed the door and padded downstairs.

She knew where Henry was by the odor in the house. Judith did not mind her husband's recreational drug use so long as it was kept away from Penny. It calmed him, or at least he thought it did. She noticed little difference between high Henry and regular Henry except his infrequent smiles turned to laughter a little easier.

"Is it helping?" she asked from the cracked doorway.

The joint glowed for a second, faint smoke swirling toward the fan. Judith stepped onto the deck so the smoke would not trickle inside.

"Mmph."

"Guessing you watched more news? Any reason for it yet?"

"It?"

"The ships. Whatever else is going on…"

Henry inhaled again. He always smoked in the dark, was afraid neighbors would see him and turn him into the police. Judging by the smell outside on nights he was not smoking, his neighbors would have been hypocrites to report him.

"No reason. Everyone is just guessing."

She nodded, "Any good guesses?"

Henry pinched the end of the joint, seethed, and placed it on the wicker table.

"Well, there's one word that keeps coming up. I don't think it fits."

Judith walked forward a few paces, gripped the chair facing her husband.

"What's that?"

"Terrorism," he scoffed.

"You don't think it is?"

He shook his head.

"Then…" Judith began.

"I don't know. I don't wanna find out."

Judith bit the inside of her cheek. He was making this about him. Whatever this was. Henry had found a way to make it about him again. How many times had they play-acted this ritual? Henry shutting down, forgetting he was a dad until it was convenient for him to remember. She had been the soft place to fall so many times she felt her stuffing was not so buoyant, not enough for both of them.

"What is that?"

She nodded at the uniform draped over the rocking chair next to him.

"Is that your…" she trailed off.

Henry retrieved it, held it up as if he forgot it was there. It smelled of propellant and copper.

Judith took a step back, her eyes focused on the dark splotch interrupting the camo pattern. She grasped the doorknob.

"Don't worry. It's not my blood, remember?" Henry said.

Maybe it should have been.

She hated herself for the thought. But she hated him more in that moment. Judith had a past, too, trauma wearing the mask of a loved one. But she didn't put his fucking picture on the coffee table.

"Don't forget, you have to be a father tomorrow. A couple of ships sinking doesn't change that."

Judith shut the door with more force than was needed. It felt good to do it.

***

Henry considered relighting the joint. He sniffed it, rolled it between his fingers. With his other hand he scratched the scars beneath his shirt. They no longer hurt, but they sure could itch.

He pocketed the joint, intending to dispose of it once inside. The weed was not having its desired effect. Instead of calm he felt less in control of his thoughts. For a person whose thoughts could wander into dark alleys, that was not a good thing.

Years ago, he would have run after Judith. He would have apologized without understanding the infraction. She had put the pieces of him back together, reassembled them each time the stitching came loose. But after putting Henry back together dozens, maybe hundreds of times, she no longer had the skill for it. Her attempts were haphazard, rushed, incomplete. Weed didn't hold him together, but it helped not to think about the reasons he'd come undone. Not that night, however.

Henry stepped onto the backyard grass glowing blue-gray in the moonlight. This was not their dream home, but a bridge to it. They intended to raise a family here. The dream home would come later. The schools were good. It was safe. It was also a growing source of Henry's anxiety. From where he stood, he could see the backyards of fifteen other houses. Three trampolines, two rubber pools, six sheds. Two houses to his left, a neighbor was attempting to coax her Rottweiler back inside. A bit further away, someone was practicing the drums in their garage.

At least they had not moved next to the drummer. Small miracles.

For its safety it did not feel like a community. Of the people Henry waved to while walking with Penny through the neighborhood, he could only have named the man across the street and that was because their mail was often mixed up.

Henry's gaze fell upon something he could not immediately identify. He scaled the steps to the deck to get a better view. Maybe it was a tree, a sapling? He squinted, cupped his hands around his eyes but saw no clearer.

"Oh," Henry said, and pulled his cell phone out of his pocket.

He opened the camera and swiped his fingers to zoom. It was difficult to keep in frame, but Henry was quite certain the image on his screen was of a woman. She wore a sports bra and sweatpants. Though it was a mild night for January even by south Texas standards, it was not bra weather.

"What are you doing?" he whispered, glancing from the screen to the woman several backyards away.

Her head was cocked back, mouth agape, blunted tip of her nose aimed at the moon or somewhere near it. The slight breeze lifted her hair, but otherwise she was mannequin-still. Both arms were limp by her sides. Though she did not appear to be in distress there was a tautness to her posture, a rigidness to her curved neck, like a bow drawn to its limit.

A minute passed, then two. Henry scratched his chest, willing the woman to move.

Was anyone else seeing this?

He scanned the backyards, with purpose this time.

"Oh, fuck."

His backyard neighbor, a man whose name he did not know but whose children called him *Papa*, was standing in the grass, head cocked and mouth open. Henry did not need his phone to see him clearly. He looked as if he'd been snatched from a deep sleep, hair flattened by his pillow, eyes half-lidded.

Henry pressed a hand to his chest, felt his heart thrum like a tuning fork. Once he had felt this lost before, this confused. With the tickle of foreign dust in his nose and a thousand needles in his chest he became a bystander to himself, a spectator to his own suffering. The specter and the body were rejoined, but not fully. The borders of one often bled free from the other. In that sense, Judith's efforts to stitch him together only delayed the inevitable.

You have to be a father tomorrow.

Henry turned his back on his neighbor, his wife's words louder than the rush of blood in his ears.

If I am one thing it is that.

He knew Judith was pretending to sleep. She always slept on her side, not her back. Henry eased beneath the blankets, upholding her ruse. He wanted to tell her what was happening outside but did not have the words to frame it. He wanted to take her hand and place it on his chest, let her feel the terror vibrating there. He wanted to commiserate with her as a husband to a wife.

Judith didn't need a husband, not then. She needed a father for her daughter. Henry rolled onto his side, felt the slight shift as his wife turned his direction. Maybe there were words she wanted to tell him. Maybe she wanted to reach across the cold distance between them.

If so, the words went unspoken, and the distance between them was a long December night. The mattress shifted again, comforter pulling tight as Judith turned to go to sleep.

Henry counted her breaths until sleep claimed her. He allowed five more minutes to pass, then slid out of the bed and crossed the room on mouse paws. He parted the blinds and watched the man he only knew as Papa gawk at constellations overhead, mouth open as if preparing to receive rain from a mostly cloudless sky.

A gunshot nearby. The blinds snapped back into place and Judith sucked in a deeper breath but did not rouse. Henry touched his chest again, fingertips tracing the lunar

31

terrain of old wounds. Two more gunshots a bit further away. His breath fogged the window glass as he parted the blinds again.

    Papa stared, waited for rain.
    Henry returned to the bed.
    He had to be a father again in the morning.

"I Followed a Stargazer and This is What Happened"

31 January 2023, 1:45 AM User – **ColoradoKid_14:**

I've been tracking these threads for a couple of days. Thought it was some shared universe experiment by the writers in the group. I found it fun, different. Lots of ideas get recycled here so it was cool to see something new even if the stories were sort of pointless. No offense to the authors. By pointless I mean they didn't have a real ending.

Well, it may not be an ending, but I have more to add to the story. I truly thought it was fiction until I went out to my truck yesterday morning. I like to hit the gym before the crowds get there, which means I'm on the road at the ass-crack of dawn. I was surprised to see my neighbor, Eric, standing outside. I don't recall ever seeing him up that early.

Wasn't too interested in striking up a conversation, but I said hello and commented on how early it was. He didn't respond, which was strange. Eric's one of those overly friendly neighbors, the kind who thinks personal space is more of a suggestion than a rule. I can't count the number of times he's trapped me in a conversation that went absolutely nowhere but took a thousand side roads to get there.

I tossed my gym bag in the passenger seat and popped my head back out.

"Eric? You okay, buddy?" I asked.

He was just like the others described in this forum. Mouth open, head tilted back. He wore a robe and pajamas. By the redness of his nose and cheeks, revealed by the porch-light, it was apparent he'd been standing there for some time.

I'm going to upload a picture of him at the end of this post. Normally, I wouldn't do that. He didn't give permission, but that's sort of a moot point now.

Had I not read what I thought were stories discussing this exact phenomenon I probably would have done more to rouse him. I at least would have picked him up, or attempted to, and taken him inside.

The title of this thread is "I Followed..." and that's only somewhat misleading. I have no fucking idea what is going on in the world right now. You've all seen the news. But until they tell me to stop coming in I have a job to go to. I don't think my boss would excuse me because my neighbor turned into stone.

What I mean to say is, I didn't follow him. I went to the gym and tried not to think about it. What I did do was place one of those little trackers people fix to their luggage or whatever. Mine was on the case of my work cell phone.

This is longer than I thought it would be and I apologize if it isn't all that interesting. Bear with me.

Couldn't really get into my workout. On the TV there was the news about all those cell phone towers being taken down on screen and more ships being sunk on another. The other early birds were just standing around. No squat records were set that morning. I half-assed it through the workout and checked the tracking app on my phone after getting out of the shower.

Eric was on the move. He was still in the neighborhood, but he was moving.

I got little work done the rest of the day, not that anyone is paying attention right now. Eric did not stop moving. I tracked him all day. He followed streets that progressively became more rural. Around dinner time he was off the map, meaning the app only showed white space around him, no roads.

In bed, I read every thread about Stargazers. I watched the videos. It was no longer entertaining, no longer fun. No post mentioned where they went. And after walking all day, Eric had finally stopped.

*I couldn't sleep without finding out. Fuck the gym tomorrow. I needed to know where Eric went. Took me two hours to get there. I'll spare the details of that journey except to say I am glad I have a four-wheel drive. Where is **there**? Nowhere, really. It's one of those spaces in between on the map, five miles west of the interstate in a field probably used for cattle grazing.*

*There were maybe a thousand of them. Maybe more. I can't say I'm good at estimating crowd sizes, but **a lot**, I'll leave it at that.*

What would you guess they were doing?

Yep.

*Picture it. A thousand people lit by **your** headlights, staring at the sky. A thousand open mouths. A thousand bent necks.*

Fuck yes I got out of there.

What I hadn't noticed driving in, too focused on not driving off a cliff, was that not everyone made it. I passed a woman caught in a barbed wire fence. The skin of her arm rolled back from her elbow like a sleeve. De-gloving I think it's called? She was still pulling to get free. And she felt it. Her expression never changed. It was something I saw in her eyes.

There were others. A dead man I nearly ran over and a smaller body nearby I'd rather not think about.

Friends, I'm going rural and you should too. Fuck the job. Fuck my boss. If you can think of a positive outcome from all of this chaos feel free to share.

I won't read it. I'm out.

31 January 2023, 2:11 AM - User **Danightstalka595:**

Now that's a story! The other authors on this page could learn from this one.

31 January 2023, 2:15 AM – User **HydroSportLuvrr:**

Nightstalka don't you have anything better to do than comment on every fucking thread. Here's an idea. Ask your mom to get the shovel, the big one with the thick handle, to pry you out of that basement recliner your fat ass melted into. Go outside. Now. While it's still dark. Take a look around. I just did and guess what? I'm taking OP's advice.

CHAPTER THREE – FALLS APART

"Should I reschedule?" Judith asked.

She stood in front of yesterday's presentation. Instead of a dozen pairs of white or silver eyebrows there were two. The hospital administrator sighed, not for laughs. The doctor to his left held his cell phone two inches from his nose and shook his head in disbelief every few seconds.

"I, uh, don't think that's necessary, Mrs. Sylva."

"Sir, I…"

He held up a hand, "Call me Dan. No need to be formal now."

"Sir, Dan, do you know anything? Is it medical? A mass psychosis?"

The doctor looked up from his cell phone, "Not possible."

"Well then…" Judith began.

"You have a family, Mrs. Sylva? You mentioned a husband yesterday?" Dan asked.

She nodded, "Judith, if we're not being formal."

"We are the largest hospital system in the seventh biggest city in the country. We treat thousands of patients every day."

Judith nodded.

Dan removed his glasses, rubbed his eyes with his thumbs.

"I was here on 9/11. Logistics at that time. It was all hands on deck. New York is fifteen hundred miles away and we were getting hourly updates. America was attacked and who was to say it would stop at New York and DC? We needed to stock up on blood. We had police patrolling the hallways. We were preparing for war because we were attacked."

Judith nodded again.

"This? Nothing. We've heard nothing. Nothing about the cell phone towers. Nothing about the dead bodies on the side of the road, the people walking like…like they're hypnotized."

"What does-" she began.

Dan held a hand up, "It means we weren't attacked, not in the traditional sense. Something happened. Something *is* happening, but it's not something we can repel with missiles. You have a family. That is your priority now."

Judith nodded.

"Be with them. Maybe there's something on the other side of this. If there is, I'd love nothing more than for you to finish your briefing. Until then, I have to go. My family is out of state. It's probably not the best idea to be on the road now, but I'll take my chances."

***

"Daddy, where are all those people going?" Penny asked, straining against the belts pinning her to the car seat.

Henry feared the enamel of his teeth might fracture, fragment into shards leaving behind trembling roots, but he could not unclench his jaw. He found his daughter's eyes in the rearview mirror as she waved, blew him kisses. He molded his lips into a smile, hoped that would suffice for the moment.

"There's lots of people! Wonder where they're goin'?"

Henry nodded, "Mmmhmmm."

This was a bad idea. He hadn't realized it when loading Penny into the SUV. The neighborhood felt a bit different at a quick glance. Open front doors and garages. It was trash day but there were only a few bins on the curb. Earlier, Henry had relinquished control of the television to his daughter. One minute of news coverage was enough. He had a single goal for the day, to be a father to Penny. The news turned him into something else.

But the push notifications kept coming, and the *ding* was the same sound as an incoming text message. As Penny flitted, butterfly-like, around the living room, Henry scrolled through headlines. The sunken aircraft carriers were a lifetime ago compared to what had happened since. Dams and bridges destroyed, buildings demolished. While scrolling, a new term caught his eye.

Stargazers

He shuddered, the image of *Papa* still as a corpse fresh in his mind. The strange encounter from the night before was not an isolated event. The first few Stargazer videos went viral, but now there were thousands. There was drone footage of masses of people huddled in fields or parking lots. Other videos showed the Stargazers tearing the infrastructure of their communities apart, with tools or their bare hands. Whatever afflicted them made the efforts imprecise, but what they lacked in skill they made up for in relentlessness. There were bodies in the streets, Stargazers claimed by the elements.

Power went out mid-morning. Though it returned within minutes the uncomfortable silence, punctuated by gasps of boredom from Penny, prompted Henry to inspect the refrigerator and then the pantry. There wasn't enough food. He didn't know how much qualified as *enough*, but it was more than they had. Texans could clean out a grocery store if flurries were in the forecast. Henry was behind.

"Why they dressed like it's summer?" Penny chirped. Still fighting the straps.

They hadn't made it out of the subdivision and Henry was close to shutting down. There was too much information, too many possibilities blossoming in his mind. On the sidewalks and staggering through the streets were dozens of neighbors, none he knew personally, though he recognized a few faces from the park or pool. Some were evacuating. Some were just walking. Some were attempting to convince the walkers to evacuate.

There were screams from glass-filled throats. Gunshots Henry convinced Penny were only fireworks. On the corner of Cactus Way, a man with a rifle sat on his porch, aiming the weapon at each person or car that passed. His boots were propped on a cooler and a Modelo rested against his belly.

"I don't think they know that it's not summer," Henry said, mouth as dry as shoe leather.

He drove past the man on the porch without looking his direction, could feel the rifle's sight follow him down the street.

"Why not? Oh! Hey, that's Riley's mom! Why she in her underwear? Can you stop and I can ask?"

Henry gritted his teeth, checked the side mirror. The rifle acquired a new target.

"No, honey. We have to get to the store."

His voice felt pubescent, like he couldn't hold enough air in his diaphragm to form the words.

"Why? What's goin' on at the store? Is that where everyone's goin'?"

Henry shook his head, "I don't think so."

"Maybe it's the food truck? That only comes on Friday. Is it Friday?"

Henry switched on the radio.

"No, it's not Friday."

There was only static, so he turned it off.

"Oh, shit," he said.

"Daddy that's a bad word!"

"Penny, listen to me. I need you to look at your shoes, okay? Look at your shoes until I tell you to look up. Tell me about them. What color are they?"

The woman had been stripped naked. The man walking behind her stroked his erect penis, her clothes draped over his shoulder. With his free hand he pressed her underwear to his nose. He bit them and grabbed her, clawed her skin. She kept walking, bloody footprints trailing behind.

"The end parts are a little scuffy 'cause I like to run real fast outside. But they're s'posed to be white. Um, there's stripes on the side…"

The fear building inside of him bubbled into rage. He pictured himself beating the man, stomping his dick into the concrete until it was only gray paste. But to do that he would have to park. He would have to leave Penny. Still, he slowed, let the man hear the rumble of his engine, and he did. He stopped in his pursuit, underwear spilling out of his mouth. He broke eye contact with Henry and focused on the shoes flutter-kicking in the backseat.

"…straps but some of my shoes have laces. Daddy can I look now?"

The engine roared. Maybe that would be enough. To let the predator know he had been seen.

"Yes, but just look at me, okay? Just look forward."

What the fuck was happening? He reached for his cell phone. No service. There was still Internet in the house, but his phone was useless once out of range of Wi-Fi.

He couldn't stop, couldn't summon help. He could only move forward. More neighbors, more screams pleading for them to stop. Blood on the sidewalk. A woman holding a screaming toddler, legs taut as a teenage girl tried to wrestle it from her grasp.

Henry eased out of the subdivision, the color draining from his rigid knuckles as though to loosen his grip on the steering wheel might send him rocketing through the windshield. The traffic lights were out. Vehicles crept through the intersection, weaving around Stargazers, but not all drivers had been so careful.

Henry gasped. He felt his bones come unmoored from muscles and tendons. His brow tingled. The scars on his chest sparked to life.

"Fuck. Fuck. Fuck…" he whispered.

"Daddy that's a really bad word!"

The man had been struck by a vehicle. By the devastation to his legs it could have been a semi. He dragged the pulpy remnants of his lower half over the sidewalk, white flecks of bone peeking through tatters of flesh and arteries belching bright red blood. With his forearms, he pulled himself in the direction the others walked.

The man's silver hair and bright olive skin reminded Henry of his father. The boy following the man, screaming for him to stop, reminded Henry of himself as a child. Raven hair butchered into a flattop, dollar store Rustlers sliding past his hips. From her perspective, Penny couldn't see the boy or his father, the viscera fanning from his knees like a bloody mermaid's tail.

"I said that's a really bad word, Daddy!"

She furrowed her brows at him, wagged a finger.

"But Mommy says it," he replied. He had to keep her engaged, distracted. He forced breaths between the gaps in his teeth.

Rain pinged on the windshield. Henry switched on the wipers.

"But *you* don't, Daddy. *You* don't say those words."

The rain would not be good for them, the Stargazers. They were mostly dressed for bed, nightgowns, boxer shorts and baggy t-shirts. Though it was a Texas winter it was still winter.

"I'm not allowed?"

Penny thought for a moment, "I guess if you need to. But you can use other words like..."

"Like what?"

"Like potato!"

"Okay. I'll try to say potato from now on."

Penny sank into her car seat, satisfied. Henry pulled up a game on his cell phone, offered it to Penny.

"I'm not s'posed to play on the phone."

"It's okay," Henry said, smiling at the rearview mirror. "Just for now."

"Oh, yay!" she said, taking it from him.

He returned his attention to the street, mostly clear save for a few stragglers on the shoulder. They walked with purpose. Those that staggered or stumbled did so from injury. Many, if not most were barefoot, glass and gravel like barnacles hitching a ride in the soft flesh of their feet. They were not zombies. They were *compelled*. To what purpose? Henry could not even guess.

He passed a strip mall comprised of a dentist's office, boxing gym, and a liquor store. The latter was in the process of being raided though not violently. A team of three men hoisted a keg into the bed of a small truck as liquor bottles were passed, fire brigade style, to waiting cars. Henry considered stopping for gas at the service station ahead. There were no cars at the pumps and only one vehicle parked in front of the store. Then he noticed the man on the roof, rifle held at low-ready. He kept driving.

The nearest grocery store was a mile up the road, with a few strip malls and an apartment complex before it. He could make the drive in his sleep, but a nightmare overlaid it at that moment, bloody footprints on the asphalt, a parade of neighbors marching toward an unknowable future. Children dug their heels into the ground, tugged the limp wrists of their unwavering parents.

There was a steady stream of traffic in the opposite lane, headed out of the city, cars and vans loaded with luggage, truck beds overflowing. Was that the answer? Flee the city? If so, they would need supplies and where was Judith? He couldn't leave without her.

Old memories roused from the basement of his mind like an October wind breathing life into a scattering of leaves. He smelled the exhaust and the blood, some of it his own. Henry sat taller in his seat, chin hovering over the steering wheel. The drone of asphalt beneath his tires became the whirr of a helicopter's rotors. That place, that memory felt more real than the world before him. Hundreds of people in pajamas abandoning the city like some spontaneous, human migration.

"Potato!"

Henry jolted.

"What?" he said.

"Potato potato! This potato game is too hard!"

He blinked, took another breath. The sound of his daughter's voice was a beacon in the darkness.

"Keep trying, hon. Show that potato game who's boss."

A truck two blocks ahead came to a jolting stop. Henry pressed the brake, slowing his speed. After a few seconds, the truck peeled out, hopped the concrete median and flew down the road in the opposite direction.

"What the f-..." Henry whispered, glancing in the rearview. Penny's tongue was out, eyes squinting in concentration.

He eased forward, chin back over the steering wheel. "What is..."

There was a man standing in the road. Beyond him and along the shoulder were bodies, ten or more. The street shimmered, a dull sun peeking through sporadic clouds to reflect off swelling pools of blood. He was shirtless, back turned to Henry for a moment, gun held limply against his thigh. The grocery store was half a block beyond the carnage, the parking lot almost empty.

Henry could not reach it without putting bodies under his tires. He stopped, prompting Penny to look up from the phone.

"What is it, Daddy?"

The man in the street turned. He nodded, began sprinting toward the SUV. Wet blood streaked his face like warpaint.

"Oh shit," Henry said.

For its oversized tires, the SUV wasn't all that nimble. Hitting the median at an angle sent the vehicle skidding back into the street. The man waved his gun in the air, thrashed his other hand as if swatting hornets.

"They're all infected! I got 'em! They're all infected!" he screamed.

The man's torso was a single-color Pollock. He slapped the hood of the SUV, leaned against it, and smiled. It was a smile of commiseration, a *can you believe this* smile.

"Daddy?"

Henry held up one finger, out of the man's sight.

"I fuckin' got 'em. I fuckin' took 'em out before they could infect us."

Henry nodded.

The man placed the gun, its barrel aimed at Henry's chest, on the hood. He wiped blood from his brow, smeared it on his jeans.

"Daddy!"

The man flinched, followed the sound of Penny's voice. He retrieved the weapon and walked to the side of the vehicle, pressed his face to the window.

"Hello small fry!" the man said, waving.

Penny said nothing. She stared.

"Hey!" Henry barked, startling the shirtless man.

He stood beside the passenger window, gun out of sight. His lips were pulled into a tight line, the commiserating smile gone. He squinted, eyes crawling over Henry's body.

"Seen some of 'em using vehicles downtown. It makes 'em crazy, makes 'em destroy things," the man said, resting the gun along his forearm. "Got a certain look to 'em, you know? Around the eyes."

His finger tapped the grip of the gun and Henry stared straight forward.

"They're killin' their own. You know that? One of those overpasses in the city. Mamas tossin' their babies over. Pile of babies got so tall it wasn't killin' 'em to land on it, not enough distance. They just rolled down the mountain, and landed in the street. Can you imagine that?"

Henry swallowed, briefly made eye contact.

"Where you goin' with that young'un? Where you takin' her?" the man asked, motioning with the gun. "You drivin' into the city, to the overpass?"

"Daddy? What's wrong with that man?" Penny asked, holding the cell phone to her tiny chest.

Henry shook his head. Could he drive away fast enough? He couldn't run him over if he wanted. The man took a step back, raised his weapon. Sludge pumped through Henry's veins, a thousand outcomes vying for space in his mind.

"There!" Henry yelled, pointing.

The man followed the direction Henry indicated. A cluster of Stargazers approached the bodies of their fallen ilk, though the newly dead were not their goal. They stepped, barefoot, into puddles of still warm blood, unblinking.

The moment the man's attention diverted Henry reversed the SUV and slammed into the median head on. Penny screamed from the impact as the SUV launched into the outbound lanes. The cell phone became a missile.

"Daddy!!" she cried.

Tires screeched as Henry joined the convoy of vehicles headed out of the city. Time slowed, as it had once before, and Henry was able to see the gun-wielding stranger in his peripheral vision. The weapon was aimed at a woman attempting to regain her footing after slipping in a puddle of blood. The bottom half of her pink robe was red, dripping. In that moment she possessed the will, but not the skill to right herself. Instead, she floundered, like a catfish trapped in a shriveling summer pool. He pressed the barrel to her head.

CLICK

Henry didn't hear it, couldn't hear anything above Penny's cries, but he knew the sound it made. The man tried again. Same result. He flipped the gun, holding the barrel, and raised it above her head.

Henry did not watch. He unleashed thunder, all those seldom-tasked horses under the hood. They careened past minivans, clover noses of children pressed to the windows. Penny screamed, balled her hands into fists and pummeled the arms of her car seat.

"Gotta get home Penny! Don't look! Just, don't look! Gotta get home, gotta get home, gotta get home..."

Mania crept into his voice, stole the reason and credibility from it. Penny's fists found new purpose, to dam the tears flowing from her eyes. She knew how to pull her father from his dark, private places. She knew the words to say, a little dance she could do or face she could make. But he was not lost, not in the same way he had been before.

The SUV streaked through an intersection, the wind of its passage rustling the nightgown of a Stargazer angling for the shoulder. Up ahead and to the left, the man with the ruined legs was still, belly-down on the concrete. His prematurely grayed head rested in the lap of his son, who sobbed and shook the man's shoulders. Light rain mixed with the dying man's blood, turning it into rivers that ran into the storm drain.

The tires skipped and skidded over the slick asphalt as Henry careened to the right. Penny shrieked, pulled her knees to her chest as best she could manage.

"It's okay, baby! It's okay! Gotta get home. Just gotta…"

He turned into the subdivision, distracted for a moment by the naked woman from earlier. It felt like hours ago but was likely no more than ten minutes. She walked alone, her attacker gone. Turning down another street Henry learned his fate.

Josh, Henry thought his name was. He recalled meeting him at the food truck a handful of times. Josh's kids liked to harvest crawdads from the pond and often let Penny net them if she was around. He was an Army veteran, but they never talked about it, never talked about where they'd been or what they'd done. The novelty shirts they picked up along the way told the story. *I Survived Camp X* or *120 degrees in the shade, but it's a dry heat!*

Henry slowed, rolled down the window.

"Josh?"

"Hey buddy," he replied, shifting the baseball bat to his other shoulder.

Henry's gaze fell to the twitching body at Josh's feet.

"Had to do it," Josh said. "Things are goin' to shit, man. Stephanie is gone. So are the kids. Heard some rumors that, well, I can't even think about it right now. But, at least I got this fucker."

Henry nodded, "You leaving?"

Josh shrugged, "Don't know what to do. Guessing Steph went wherever the, uh, star people, are headed. Maybe I can follow them and find her."

Henry nodded, "I won't stand in your way. Good luck out there."

"You too. And, hey, if you see me wandering around like one of them," he said, pointing to a man in yellow spotted tighty-whities on the sidewalk. "Just make it quick."

***

The text messages dinged as soon as Henry was within range of Wi-Fi.

Leaving work. Things are getting bad. Stay home with Penny, okay?

You there? They let me take food from the cafeteria. Will need help unloading.

Oh my God. They're demolishing the city…bodies in the streets. What is happening?!? Please tell me you didn't leave!!

Your phone is going straight to voicemail! Answer me please!!!

Before he could respond, Henry had to be a father. He situated Penny with a juice box and peanut butter crackers, played a Disney movie with an earworm of a soundtrack he hoped might insulate her from recent memories. As he began to compose a response, he heard a car door slam. Keys rattled in the lock and then Judith spilled through the front door, falling to her knees and shutting the door behind. She collapsed onto her side, pulled her knees to her chest as Henry darted to her side.

"It's okay," he said, draping his warmth over her body, shivering like a newborn kitten.

She screamed into the fabric of his jeans, legs stiff as stilts. She screamed again and again, head lolling, fists like mallets.

"No it's not! It's fucking not!"

Is this what it was like for her? Henry's breakdowns were mostly quiet, subtle, like a boat slipping loose of its moorings to drift unguided on the sea. She hardened as he held her, her elbows creating space between them.

"What happened out there? What did you see?" Henry asked.

She scooted away from him, placed her back to the front door.

"Is she okay?" Judith asked, avoiding his questions.

"Penny? Yes, she's probably going to crash soon. We had a rough time out-"

"You went out!?"

Henry held up his hands, "We needed food. We still do."

She sighed, neck bent under the weight of her thoughts.

"Judy?"

She sniffed, wiped her nose. Not all of Henry came back. Parts of him were frozen in time, petrified beneath the warmth of another sun. New parts emerged to take their place, new habits and methods of coping. He was not the same man, never would be. But she was not the same woman. Those soft places she once offered to him freely grew callouses, so dense she couldn't even sense his feather-light touches, probing for comfort and peace.

What she had seen in the past thirty minutes would change her forever, she knew. What had Henry seen over all those months?

"What are we gonna do, Henry?" she whispered, her hand finding his.

She allowed him to gather her limbs and fold her into his chest. But he did not answer. He had no answer for her.

**

In the evening, Henry found Penny asleep on the floor of her bedroom, a stuffed animal in one hand and a half-eaten apple in the other. He hoisted her onto her bed, pulled the blankets to her chin as she turned on her side.

"Should we leave her up there?" Judith asked.

Henry secured another box with packing tape.

"Probably for now. Gonna be noisy down here with all the movement. She needs sleep. I don't know how much she saw, but even a little was too much."

They had decided to evacuate. No one understood the goal of the Stargazers beyond destroying the infrastructure of the civilized world. Those not involved in the destruction massed in open spaces as if awaiting inspiration for the next action. By Judith's estimation, the devastation was spreading outward from the city's center, meaning the suburbs would also be leveled. Gunfire fractured their communication, screams both near and far away. Dogs barked incessantly, and Henry wondered how many were left alone, left in kennels never to be opened, behind fences they would never see beyond.

"There were men ramming bulldozers into that tower, the one with the restaurant on top? Chipping away at it. Wasn't all that efficient, but I guess it'll get the job done eventually. The thing is, they're going to be buried. When the tower does fall they'll be under the rubble," Judith said, flinching at each new volley of gunfire.

"I don't know if that matters to them," Henry said.

The electricity flickered throughout the evening, smoke alarms chirping back to life each time it returned. Penny slept through it all, somehow, as her parents packed the SUV leaving only the food to deal with in the morning.

They took hot showers, the weight of the day like anchors in their hearts. In bed, Judith pressed her body into his for the first time in years.

"Feels like we should be doing something, you know? The world is on fire and we're just...going to bed," Judith said, her cheek resting against Henry's belly.

"Whatever comes tomorrow we'll need to be rested," Henry replied in a monotone voice.

"What is it?" Judith asked.

Henry offered his phone.

"What am I looking at?" she asked.

"Drone footage I think."

"Of what?"

She squinted but could not make sense of the images.

Henry touched the bottom half of the screen, "That's the ocean," he said, then moved his finger. "Those are people."

Judith swallowed, tried to pass the phone back to him.

"What are they doing?"

Henry placed the phone face down on the comforter. Outside the walls of their cookie-cutter house the world was unraveling. The soundtrack swelled and subsided, like a rising tide crawling toward beach grass only to submit to gravity, goal unrealized. The video was a dagger that ruptured each of his defenses, planted its tip in the very center of his soul. The effect was not panic, but a growing numbness, veins and arteries filled with Lidocaine. He could not imagine anything worse than the video on his phone.

"They're walking their children into the sea."

As if a dumbbell had been dropped on her stomach, Judith gasped and retrieved the phone. The camera zoomed so that only a few dozen people were captured. Mothers, mostly, children in arms, sometimes two or three of them. They walked into the cold ocean only wavering if a wriggling child slipped free. The mothers corralled them as if gathering laundry and continued into the water. Judith fixated on one individual. The water lapped at her shoulders as little hands clawed at her face from both sides. The children were not visible, just their small, desperate fingers tearing at the flesh of the woman who carried them in her womb. The water touched her chin, then her nose. Just before she went under, she closed her eyes.

There were thousands. The drone pivoted to show a view of the horizon. Hundreds of bodies drifting on tepid waves, mothers' arms entangled with the limbs of their young.

"I could never," Judith said, too stunned to cry.

Henry ran his fingers through her hair.

"I'm sure they would have said the same before," he said.

"But…but why?"

"Why are they doing it?"

"Why are they doing it? Why is this happening at all?"

Henry blinked at the paint splatter texture of the ceiling. He spent many sleepless nights finding meaning in the shapes.

"I don't know why. I can guess about some of it, how things are connected."

"What's your guess?"

"They're all Stargazers, right?"

"I mean, I haven't heard it confirmed anywhere. It's not like the government is putting out information right now."

"If that is the case, then that's the one common thing among them. Figure out what happened to them while they were…gazing and we'll have our answer."

"You think so?"

"I don't know what else it could be."

"How many of us are left I wonder…"

She nestled against his chest, ran her fingers over the impressions of raised flesh below his collarbone.

"Hard to say. About half the houses in the neighborhood are dark right now. Could be people left or they're hunkered down. I guess the real question is…how many will be left tomorrow, and the day after that?"

"I don't want to think about it."

She was beyond tired, a weariness that made her bones feel like warm butter. As she drifted to sleep she whispered, half in a dream and half in reality, "I love you."

"I love you, too," Henry said.

***

The paint splatters changed shape in the darkness, like storm clouds gathering strength. Sometimes he found meaning in their configurations, but not that night. Though he was just as weary, he had felt it before, had pushed himself beyond the demands of his body. He peeled his drooling wife of his chest and propped her head with a pillow.

The baying of dogs calling for lost masters continued as the gunfire subsided. Brief pockets of silence were disturbed by raging engines as a neighbor fled under the cover of night. Henry padded upstairs to check on Penny.

She was a sea star in an ocean of pastel blue blankets, face hidden by curtains of wavy black hair. Henry sat beside the bed, leaned his head against the mattress, and inhaled the scent of her. It was no longer a baby scent. There was a hint of salt mixed with the sweetness. But it was still her.

He knew sleep would not come for him. He was certain of it. Too much to think about. Too many plans to make. As he considered how unlikely sleep would be the reservoirs of weariness dislodged and seeped into his bloodstream. Serenaded by muffled outbursts of desperation, his thoughts about sleep slipped peacefully into it.

It was not a sound that woke him hours later. The dogs with back door splinters in the pads of their paws had not stopped howling. Slammed car doors of fleeing neighbors still broke the uneasy truces, drawing fresh barks from invigorated lungs. It was not the noise but the numbness in his legs, seated beside the bed.

To stand was an effort. His muscles filled with static. To march downstairs was a process, each step calculated, his weight hefted onto the bannister.

Though he checked the front door locks half a dozen times earlier that night, he did so then.

The door was unlocked. He saw it upon approach. How could it be?

He locked it, twisted the handle and tugged. No give. He shut one eye and peered through the peephole.
"Oh…oh no…"

"Is Anyone Out There?"

1 February 2023, 11:53 PM User – **Deadgurl_2002:**

Is anyone out there? I feel like I'm the last person on earth. I know I'm not. I can see lights in other houses. I can hear people, mostly screams far away.

If you're out there, where are you? What is happening there? Where should I go? What happened to them?

1 February 2023, 11:59 PM User – **NightWyrm666:**

I'm here OP. The east coast is going dark. I got out. Took twenty hours to make it to Tennessee. Went to my parent's farmhouse and I'm alone. Cell doesn't work out here, just the ol' reliable dial-up. Can't get in touch with my siblings but heard from a buddy in Colorado. He's off the grid now. Sounds like a good idea to me.

Seems like they're concentrating on the big cities. Closest city to me is about 3K people. It's a ghost town now but it's not on fire. Maybe it'll spread to the country. I guess we'll see.

To answer your question, bearing in mind I am just some random asshole on the Internet, you should seek non-traditional housing. A cabin in the woods will do, a tent in a pinch. Take as much as you can with you. Print out survival guides...trapping, etc. If you're a vegetarian you might need to expand your horizons 'til you can get your garden growing.

As for what happened to them...they aren't just destroying things. Yes, they're knocking buildings down, taking out bridges. But they're not leaving the shit there. Did you know that? They're moving the debris, flattening the earth.

I've done construction here and there. It's good work if you need weekend cash. I have a guess about what they're doing, but I'm reluctant to write it. I shouldn't worry about stuff like that, I know. It's the Internet not a primetime debate. But I feel like writing it might make it more true. Does that make sense?

55

Good luck OP. For anyone else out there able to read this, good luck to you as well.

2 February, 2023, 12:13 AM User – **Seehawks4eva:**

There's a small group of us heading east and north out of Seattle. If you're in the path feel free to join up. Destination is a campground in BC.

You're not alone, OP. Don't know how many of us are left, but there's still some traffic on the shortwave. Try to get your hands on one if you can. I guess the real question is how many will be left tomorrow? How many will be left a year from now?

From what I'm hearing, the destruction is not wholesale. Many landmarks are intact. Strange, isn't it? Level the city but leave the monuments. Who are they for? Could be a week or a month from now they're the only thing left to show we were here.

2 February, 2023, 12:28 AM User – **Itzbritkneebitch:**

*OP, take a look at this thread "**I Was a Failed Stargazer**" ...could be made up. If so, the author put a lot of effort into a hoax. I hope it was made up, though. It's scarier than any "true" story I've read on this forum. Good luck out there OP and to anyone else reading this. In case I go Gazin' tonight and these are the last words I ever write...Baba Booey Baba Booey!! I love you Howard!!!*

CHAPTER FOUR – THE PARTING

"**M**ommy!" Penny squealed.

Henry startled awake, fingers positioned to hold a weapon he did not possess. Pale, yellow light like watered down lemonade spilled into the room, but it was broken. Henry noticed but did not grasp the meaning of the silhouette beyond his toes, wiggling back to life inside thermal socks. It was too cold in the room. Power must have gone out. Had he slept through the damned alarm chirping every minute?

"What are you doing out there, Mommy?" Penny said.

Realization did not hit him at once. It was a piecing together of recent memories as he fought to regain control of tingling limbs. Judith. Judith standing just to the right of the rose bush she planted years ago and kept alive through brutal Texas summers and a surprise, once-in-a-generation snowstorm. The crown of Judith's head as she stared at the night sky, celestial bodies hidden behind a canopy of rumpled clouds promising rain that had already passed.

He did not attempt to break her fugue with force. He simply pressed his cheek to her back, felt the warmth of her against him. The words flowed freely, words that got lost somewhere between his head and his heart the past few years. He wrestled her limbs into a jacket, forced her feet into sturdy boots. And, because he still had to be a father, he left her there with a picture of Penny in her back pocket.

The woman turned her fist into a hammer and pounded the glass.

"Mommy!" Penny screamed, stumbling backwards.

Henry scooped the girl into his arms.

Judith would not be able to fit through the window even if she succeeded in breaking the glass. It was a porthole design and the larger window to the side of Penny's bed was inaccessible without a ladder taller than the one they owned. The glass spiderwebbed as Judith struck again. The next blow drew blood, and the light in the room turned orange.

BAM!

BAM!

Penny screamed and covered her ears.

BAM!

Blood coated the window so that only Judith's eyes were visible. Henry slammed the door and scurried downstairs.

"What's Mommy doing!? Daddy, what's happening!?"

"Shhh…gotta keep it down, sweetie. I'll explain it the best I can, but we have to leave."

"Leave? Leave Mommy? Why? What did she do?"

He sat Penny down on the kitchen island as he wheeled the cooler to the refrigerator.

"I can't explain now. We just have to get out of here."

"Where? Where we gonna go?"

Henry held up a finger, turned his ear toward the stairwell. No impacts. Where was she? Was she squeezing her body through the too small hole?

I could never…

Judith from last night could not imagine a mother walking her children into the ocean, holding their heads beneath the waves, stiffened little bodies turning to putty. But that was not Judith outside Penny's window. That was a Stargazer.

Henry packed the meals from the hospital cafeteria, dumped ice on top of them. He popped his head up, held a finger in the air as Penny sucked in a breath to ask another question he would not be able to answer.

It was a sense he cultivated in another time and place, recognition of an unnatural silence, stillness as a prelude. The gravity of a predator pulling some essential part of him.

WHAM

The living room curtains fluttered. Penny slapped her hands over her ears. Before she could summon a scream she was ferried across the kitchen and into the garage, cooler and food left behind.

"Daddy!" she cried.

WHAM

He dumped her into the car seat and closed the door.

"Daddy I'm not buckled!"

He turned the key with his right hand and nudged the garage door remote with a knuckle of his left. The garage door screeched to life. Had it always taken this long to open?

"Daddy!" Penny wailed, her uncoordinated fingers fumbling with the buckle.

Henry's hands choked the steering wheel. Three feet, four feet. Sunlight crept across the hood of the SUV. How long did it take to get from the backyard to the front? Did Stargazers run? Five feet. How much clearance did he need? He eased forward a few inches, sunlight blasting his vision.

Six feet. Henry gunned it. Tire screeched and Penny barked in surprise. He rocketed down the driveway and took a hard left.

"Mommy?" Penny said.

Henry looked over his shoulder. Judith stood in the grass, arms limp at her sides, blood from her palms staining her pajamas.

"Daddy, what's Mommy doing out there? We have to stop! We have to get Mommy!"

He swallowed, turned his attention to the road in front of him.

"Daddy…why aren't you stopping?"

59

Henry turned onto the main road leading out of the subdivision, glimpsing Judith one final time in the rearview mirror. She was walking down the driveway.

"Mommy is...Mommy is sick. Sh- she's not sick like a cold. She's sick like...like..."

"Like in here?" Penny asked, tapping her head.

Henry adjusted the rearview mirror.

"Yeah, sort of. Baby, there are a lot of things happening in the world right now I can't really explain. I can't even try."

Penny frowned, tucked her chin to her chest.

"But I want you to know I'll never leave you. Whatever happens out there in the world I'll never leave you. I'll keep you safe. Everything I do from now on is to keep you safe."

Penny returned to fiddling with the buckle. The body of the man Josh eliminated with a baseball bat was still on the sidewalk, blood blackening on the concrete. There were fewer vehicles in driveways or parked along the street than yesterday, the same number or more Stargazers on the sidewalk.

Penny sniffled, "Would you fight a bear for me?"

Henry laughed in surprise, "I would fight a dozen of them. Probably wouldn't last long but I would go down swingin'."

"Would you fight a lion?"

"Nine lions. No more, no less."

"What about a person?"

Henry filled his lungs, sank into his seat and relaxed his grip on the steering wheel, "I will do whatever it takes."

"Why?"

He pulled out of the subdivision.

"Because I love you."

"But you love Mommy. Don't you?"

Henry stopped at the intersection. There was no outbound traffic. Maybe everyone got out during the night. He had only dry goods, and the cases of water he meant to load that morning were still in the garage. Was the crazy man still patrolling the route into the city? Bashing

Stargazers with the butt of his gun? If the chaos spread from the city's center he had no choice but to head in the opposite direction.

He turned right. The man with the bloody mermaid tail was gone, as was his son. What had not washed away of him remained in the street, a ragged foot like knobs of loosely connected ginger guarded by a turkey vulture.

"Daddy, you love Mommy?"

"Yes, Penny. I do."

"Then why we leavin' her?"

Refuse littered the street, ejected from truck beds of those evacuating.

"Her kind of sick can't be fixed with medicine, sweetie. It's not something you can go to the doctor for. I don't think so, anyway."

Penny gave up on the buckle.

"You mean she's not gonna get better?"

Henry shook his head, "I don't think so. I hope I'm wrong about that. I hope they all snap out of it. If so, I'll do everything I can to bring us back together."

"But why'd it happen to her?"

"I don't know why. It's happening to a lot of people, Penny. Those people outside walking around…they're sick like Mommy."

For the first time, Henry realized he had not called his mother or any of his siblings. They had also not called him. Things moved too fast. Maybe there was a biological reason he had not become a Stargazer. Maybe it was in his blood. If so, he hoped his family undertook similar journeys in their cities. And if it was in his blood it might be in Penny's.

Henry swerved around the debris of shattered lives, a broken suitcase spilling its guts onto the road, photo albums and baby toys. He checked the mirrors, half-expecting to see his wife trailing them.

"So…so we not gonna see her again? If she doesn't get better?" Penny said.

What he could not do was build false hope, begin their new life together on a lie. As well, he could not break her spirit with the truth. It was a matter of survival. More than anything, he needed her to cooperate. Whatever was to come, this day and any they lived to see after, she had to cooperate.

"We're gonna hope. We're gonna hope with every little bit of us that something happens, and your mother is okay on the other side of it. But until then, it's you and me."

Penny folded her hands in her lap and leaned her head into the padding of her car seat. Sometimes her daddy took her on *adventures.* It was a word she didn't fully understand. It seemed to mean many things at once. An adventure could be a picnic in the park or a trip to the big boring store with all the wood and plants. She reserved judgement on *adventures* when her daddy mentioned them. Maybe this would be like that. Maybe this would be a good kind of adventure.

"Okay, Daddy," Penny said.

From where she sat, she could only see the tops of the trees and the sky beyond. Clouds were breaking apart, glimpses of baby blue peeking through here and there. She turned her attention to her buckle again.

Henry avoided the landmines of disrupted lives without thinking about it, swerving in and out of lanes, using the shoulder when needed. Where had *they* gone? Those who left in the night? How many drivers parked their cars in the road, vacated their vehicles to honor a strange urge to stare at the sky?

How far was far enough? Out of the city or out of the county? In another life, Henry entered an uneasy alliance with chaos. It was something that found him unexpectedly. He never had time to plan his response. His body did that independent of his mind. As he posed these questions to himself and others, his body only offered a fresh flare of prickling in his scar tissue.

The space between clusters of wreckage increased as he drove through the outskirts of the city. The subdivisions gave way to chunks of wilderness, the flora not dependent on human intervention usurping oaks and willows. In the semi-arid environment, much of what grew huddled close to the earth. This is how most people pictured Texas, Henry thought. Mesquite and cactus, cattle and the facilities to slaughter them.

He drove halfway into the next county having decided nothing about his future.

Keep going. Keep going. It pulsed in his ears.

Penny fell asleep minutes after securing the buckle, her triumph at conquering that small task coaxing a genuine smile from her father. The drone of the highway and Penny's snore combined as white noise that made it difficult to hold onto any thoughts.

It was his own thirst that made the decision for him. Henry reached for a water bottle that did not exist and finally took stock of his surroundings. The city and its suburbs were well behind him. Though there were still stranded vehicles parked in the road, it was mostly clear of truck bed debris.

A road sign indicated a town two miles ahead. With no plan to adhere to he decided to stop there.

***

"The Stay-Put Inn?" Henry muttered.

The sign was still lit, flickering like a dying lightning bug, but lit, nonetheless. That meant there was likely electricity in the rooms. There was also a small grocery store across the street, which was exactly what Henry needed. One truck was parked at the far end of the motel, but the lot was empty otherwise. Henry pulled into the parking space outside the door labeled *Office*.

Penny smacked her lips, "We there?"

"We're somewhere," Henry answered. "Gonna see if we can get a room here."

And then what?

Henry didn't know. He did know he would drive until the gas ran out if he didn't stop. Before opening Penny's door, he did a few sweeps of the surroundings, peeking around corners. Chalky rocks exploded underfoot as he walked, looking and listening for signs of life. There were no Stargazers in the road. He had passed thousands during his drive. Maybe they would catch up.

Despite her protests, her assertions that she was *grown*, Henry wore Penny on his hip. The office was unlocked, the door propped open by an old work boot.

"Hello?" Henry said.

It was barely larger than a closet. There were two chairs with a small table between, a plastic plant fuzzy with dust in the corner and a water dispenser with an empty jug. It felt more abandoned than it was, various papers taped to the wall, pet policies and the like, yellowed like mummy wraps. Cobwebs as thick as Halloween décor obscured the corners of the room. The door leading to the back office was also unsecured and he let himself in.

"What are you doin'?" Penny asked.

Henry rummaged through desks until he found a white card labeled *Master.* The motel was an eyesore, the blue of its vinyl siding somehow painful to look at. The signage was decades out of style, cartoonish lettering that would have been at home in one of those X-rated 70s cartoons. Still, it did boast one glimpse of modern technology in the form of keycard entry. Henry had no idea how to program a room keycard, and the computer terminal required a password to access. Hopefully, the master key was correctly labeled.

"This is our key," Henry said, pocketing it.

He scanned the room, scraps of paper with dates and dollar figures written by an unsteady hand. There was a Far Side calendar from 2018, a mug with a splash of coffee and two dead flies in it. Nothing of use for his current situation.

"We stayin' here? Is Grandma here?"

Henry blinked several times, the question stunning him into silence as only Penny seemed capable of doing.

"What? Grandma? Sweetie, why would Grandma be here?" Henry said.

She looked at her socks, sniffled, "I just thought she might be."

Henry hoisted her back onto his hip, turned her chin to face him.

"I wish she was. I wish your mommy was here, too. I don't know what's left out there—*who* is left. But, you have me."

Penny nodded.

"That doesn't mean I'll be enough. It's okay to feel sad right now. It's okay to feel sad as long as you need."

Penny rested her head where her mother had the night before.

"Like when you felt sad?"

He nodded, slowly, "Yes. I've felt sad a lot."

"I know. But you don't have to be. You have me."

***

The master key worked. Penny tested the resilience of the mattresses as Henry unloaded essentials from the SUV. They wouldn't stay long, he thought, just long enough for him to plan the next move.

"It stinks in here!" Penny said, waving a hand in front of her nose. She cleared the gap between beds with a rabbit-hop. Henry grimaced as she placed her cheek directly onto the comforter. The room did stink, of cigarettes and spilled alcohol, bleach and sweat. The carpet was spongy underfoot, as if it had been laid over wet soil.

"Baby, please..." he trailed off.

There were thousands of things he might have to deny her in the future. To deny her the simple pleasure of jumping on a bed would not be among them.

"Be safe," he said, completing the thought.

Penny squealed, "I'm like a balloon!"

Her nightgown puffed up with air as she hopped over the chasm again.

"Well, don't fly away, little balloon."

Henry closed the door, locked it, and pressed his eye to the peephole. It had been scratched so thoroughly only the color of the outside world was discernible.

"Daddy, why's the remote got a leash?" Penny asked.

"Hmm?"

She held up the remote, but it only lifted about six inches off the nightstand before the chain anchoring it went taut. Henry inhaled the stuffy air, scratched the back of his neck. Maybe he should have kept driving.

"I guess so no one steals it."

She furrowed her brow, examined the remote as if it might be something different.

"Why steal it?"

Henry shrugged, "Memento?"

Though she did not know the meaning of the word, she nodded and placed the remote on the nightstand, brows still furrowed as she considered the possibility she had been wrong about remotes her whole life. Surely a remote was not worth stealing. But if it was a *memento*, whatever that was, that made more sense.

"I'm gonna shower. Are you okay by yourself for a minute? Your books are in the laundry basket over there," Henry said, pointing.

She bounced off the bed and padded across the carpet. Henry seethed, noticing her bare feet.

"Okay, Daddy."

"Gonna leave the door open. If someone knocks I should hear it. Don't answer, though, if I don't. Just come get me. Okay?"

"Okay."

She picked through the books as if selecting produce at the grocery store, considering a cover for a few seconds before dismissing it or adding it to the pile.

In the bathroom mirror, a ghoul stared back at Henry. Shiny, purple pouches bloomed beneath its eyes. Its hair looked as though a weed eater had passed over it once or twice. Henry ran his fingers over his face and the ghoul did the same.

"Jesus…"

It was not just the poor night of sleep, the violence he personally witnessed, or the transformation of his wife into something that still looked like her but was not her. It was all of that and the great unknown hovering just beyond the limits of his vision. He was leaping onto boulders to cross a river, though the water was so high each step was an act of faith, a hope there would be something beneath his feet.

The faucet belched rust water for a few seconds before it cleared. Henry sat on the toilet, massaged his face as he waited for the water to warm. Penny's voice, repeating words to books she memorized, rose just above the volume of the running water. She would never have a normal life, Henry knew. From the moment the first person stepped outside their home to stare, thoughtlessly, at the night sky the course of every person's life was altered. It was unfair to consider only the suffering around him. Penny had not witnessed a parent get obliterated by a vehicle like the boy. And she still had him.

For now.

The water hovered between glacial and boiling, neither extreme offering the respite he craved. He stood at the rear of the tub, splashing water onto his body and rubbing the brittle bar of motel soap over his skin.

"You okay?" he called,

"I'm okay!" Penny answered.

Henry felt less clean than when he entered the shower, the soap and inability to rinse it thoroughly leaving grease paint patches on his skin. He toweled off, realized he had not brought clothes into the bathroom, and trotted toward the gym bag he packed the evening before. The carpet massaged the soles of his feet, filled the gaps between his toes in the most uncomfortable way.

"Daddy, what's that?" Penny said, looking up from her book.

Henry glanced down.

She'd seen him without his shirt before, but maybe not recently enough to have made a memory of it.

"That? They're scars."

He hid them from view momentarily, then dropped his hand.

"Did you get hurt?"

Henry nodded, "Yes I did."

"How?"

Henry had different versions of the story to tell Penny depending on her age when she inquired. None of them accommodated this almost five-year old version of her. He did not know how to frame the experience in a way she would understand, because at the core of him he did not understand it either.

"People were shooting at us."

Penny's jaw dropped, "With guns?"

Henry nodded.

"Why?"

"They were trying to kill me."

Her shock shifted to anger, eyes narrowing.

"But you're my dad!"

Henry chuckled, "This was before you, sweetie."

"Yeah, but why would they do that?"

Henry sat on the edge of the bed.

"I was with people who were trying to kill them."

"You were both trying to kill each other?" she said.

Henry shook his head, "*I* wasn't trying to kill anyone. I was trying to save people. That was my job."

She chewed on the idea for a moment, head tilting to the side, "Did it hurt?"

"Not then. I didn't realize it happened when it did. Kinda felt like a bug bite, like a bee sting or something. I was too busy doing my job. Wasn't 'til things calmed down I felt it for real."

Penny wriggled closer to him, reached her hand up then hesitated.

"Can I touch them?" she asked.

Henry nodded, "They don't hurt anymore. It itches sometimes, but it doesn't hurt."

Tiny fingertips grazed the raised skin, the color of old pennies, a few shades darker than his natural tone. She traced the outline, tongue just parting her lips.

"They're like stars," she said, tapping the largest scar cluster and then the two to either side of it. "That's you. That's Mommy. And that's me."

His chest swelled as he inhaled. He cradled the back of her head and pressed her closer to him.

"Then she's always with us, right? Wherever we go from here."

"And we're always together, huh?"

"Always."

"Building a ladder to the stars?"

2 February 2023, 9:03 AM User – **EyedsovMarch:**

*Thank you to everyone keeping these threads alive. It's easy to feel like ur the last person in the world, well, I guess the Stargazers still count as people. Or do they? There's other threads with guesses as to why and how, but I am focused on **what**. What are they doing now? I guess I'm somewhat of a practical person. There'll be time (or maybe not!) later to figure out why. **Why** doesn't keep me and my cats safe. (BTW, I let out every cat and dog I could find in my neighborhood. Most of them followed me home and I guess I didn't really think that part thru.)*

This morning, before it got light out, I put on my investigator's cap and my gumshoe boots. I climbed inside my (another word for detective, did I miss any?) car and took a drive. They aren't hard to follow. Steady stream of humanity leaving everything they knew behind. I don't fault them for it. I'm just glad I'm not one of them. (For now) Also, there was some local drone footage on the news the day before everything went to shit. Unless they'd moved from there I knew where to go.

The toughest part was not running them over. The path went off-road and my (whatever that detective word is I can't think of) car isn't exactly built for it. I was close enough to reach out and touch them for much of the trip. So sad.

I didn't realize it while driving, only when I stopped, but many of them had tools and other supplies. I think the early videos of Stargazers kinda created an image in my mind. Just, you know, a human being whose higher functions had been shut off. Just walking.

I parked and watched. It was an open field. I think in the drone shots there were some trees, but those were gone. Couldn't guess how many of them were out there, but they weren't just standing around. Some were, those on the outskirts. I climbed on the hood of my car but couldn't see much.

But I could hear it.

It was like walking past an active construction zone times a lot.

I didn't feel comfortable entering the crowd. Could you imagine all of them turning their attention on you at the same time? Ugh, gives me chills.

Sorry if the title of this seemed like a bait and switch. I have no idea if they're building a ladder to the stars. Seems impractical, but I did see one of them attempt to demolish a post office with his bare hands. Final score for that encounter: Bricks 1 Stargazer 0.

What could they be building? Any guesses? If anyone says Taco Bell I'm deleting this thread!!!

2 February 2023, 9:08 AM User – **Notmyrealname0584:**

Taco Bell

2 February 2023, 9:11 AM User – **MollyMollyOk:**

Taco Bell

2 February 2023, 9:32 AM User – **YossarianLives!:**

Taco Bell

2 February 2023, 10:46 AM User – **DreamWeavur09:**

Taco Bell

2 February 2023, 12:32 PM User – **OfficialNoSleep:**

Taco Bueno

CHAPTER FIVE – FORAGE

Henry wanted to wake her, to tell Penny not to open the door for anyone, absolutely anyone. He had a keycard and would let himself in. She slept through his initial attempts to rouse her, a gentle nudge of the shoulders, a soft breath on her cheek. The third and fourth attempts were met with groans and claw hands.

He stood by the door, cracked open to let in a band of white light. It was quiet out there, only an occasional dog's bellow no other dog responded to. He considered carrying her to the grocery store but decided she was safer in the room. A man with a small child in his arms might have been an attractive target for a certain kind of person.

The door clicked shut behind him, the electronic lock engaging half a second later. He turned the knob, put his shoulder into the door without ramming it. No give, not even a creak of flexing wood. Henry scanned the parking lot, the road passing between it and the grocery store. No movement, and only the sound of air conditioners humming to life as the mild winter day edged toward a warm one. The truck was still parked at the far end of the lot, an old Ford single cab.

Likely, its occupant had taken an unplanned midnight walk and never returned, but Henry knew things weren't always what they seemed, that a garbage bag on the side of the road could sometimes explode. He checked his watch. Ten minutes total. That was all the time he allowed himself. Penny often crashed for several hours on the rare occasions she took an afternoon nap. He would have ample time to stock up and plan the next move.

The driver's side window was rolled down, the rough fabric of the seat dark from precipitation. It smelled of dust and hay. A bag of pickle-flavored sunflower seeds occupied the passenger seat, but nothing further could be gleaned about the truck's owner. The bed was empty save for a few rusted Bud Light cans. Henry pressed his ear to the door of the motel room directly in front of the truck. No sounds of movement from within, just the air conditioning rattling to life in the adjoining room.

Eight minutes.

"Shit," Henry muttered, and jogged across the parking lot. He looked both ways before crossing, then snickered at himself. Of course there was no traffic.

The supermarket was about the size of the countless dollar stores back in the city. That was okay. He didn't need variety, just the basics. Henry wrangled a loose shopping cart and ushered it toward the entrance. The cart's rickety wheels pulled him in opposite directions but settled upon touching the smooth concrete leading into the store.

The doors whooshed open and Henry stopped on the ragged weather mat inside. He winced. The music was painfully loud yacht rock. Not the worst music in the world, but the speakers were not designed for the volume at which they blared. The shelves were in a moderate state of disarray, but there was enough to choose from.

Seven minutes. His nose twitched. Cigarette smoke, but he sensed no threat behind it.

Penny ate about ten food items reliably, most of them shelf stable. It made little sense to burden them with items requiring refrigeration. Finding ice would be a chore future Henry would hate him for. Fruit, water, some treats for bribing. That's what Henry needed.

The wheels rattled, cart pulling hard to the left. Henry followed it as the meager produce selection was that direction. Compared to the rest of the store, the produce was mostly intact with the barren potato shelf the only exception. Henry grabbed two bags of apples and one bag of oranges. He paused beside the avocados, stomach rumbling to life. As an evacuation food it did not make sense, would likely rot in the trunk before he could eat it.

Six minutes.

"Oh, shit," he said, abandoning the avocados and wrangling the cart away from the produce.

Would Penny know what to do if she woke up and he was not there? He pictured her emerging from the motel room, calling for him. She would check the bathroom when he didn't answer, then she would likely head outside. Henry left the cart for a moment, jogged to the entrance. A slight rise in the terrain blocked his view of the motel parking lot, but the door to their room was closed.

Back at the cart, Henry snatched random toys off the shelves, trinkets and knockoff Barbies, coloring books and crayons. Penny enjoyed opening packages as much as playing with the toys inside. He would probably need the distraction.

He turned a corner to the aisle with drinks and snacks to find a woman seated on the floor, denim legs splayed and a cigarette held between two fingers like an afterthought. The puddle of blood in front of her was dry at its fringes but still wet toward the center, dark where it pooled in a broken tile.

Smoke issued from the cigarette in a wispy stream. She was so still, jelly eyes locked on the stain between her legs. It was such an unprecedented sight Henry could only stare. Maybe the blood was hers? Maybe she sustained a life-threatening injury and hauled her fading body to this seated position to smoke a final cigarette.

The guns complicated the scene. One was in her lap and the other on the tiles next to her thigh.

"Are you..." Henry began. *Alive* was the word he almost spoke.

Her head tilted his direction.

"I'm tryin' to quit," she said, husky voice wet with phlegm.

Henry nodded.

"Are you hurt?" he said, nearly shouting to be heard over the music.

She took a puff and then let the cigarette fall from her fingers.

"No. That's my husband's blood."

Henry swallowed, looked to his left and right. The music was so loud he would not have heard someone coming.

"Did he become one of, of *them*?"

She sighed and shook her head, "We were headed out of the city. Lookin' for a place to wait this thing out. We left with just the clothes on our backs. No food. No water. It was gettin'…nasty back there. We stopped here for supplies. Marcus made me wait in the car, said he would scope it out."

She glanced at her fingers as if expecting to find a cigarette there.

"I heard the shot, and I knew. Marcus didn't have a gun on him. Might not think it to look at me, but we're not *gun* people. I've been to the range a few times, but that's about it."

"Someone killed him?" Henry asked.

She nodded, "Guess you couldn't call him a squatter exactly. He worked for the store. Used to anyway. Probably thought he was defendin' his territory. Like I said, I knew what happened. Didn't need to come see for myself. Instead, I parked the truck, Ol' Reliable we called her, around the side and went lookin' for a weapon. Second house I checked had a gun. Guess that's Texas for ya.

That music's a good idea. Made it so Marcus didn't hear him sneakin' up, likely. But, *he* didn't hear me either. 'Cept I can't find where it's comin' from or I'd of turned it off."

"He?"

She waved her hand toward the rear of the store, "He's in the cooler back there. His body is. Big, nasty sonofabitch. He was wheelin' a mop and bucket to clean up Marcus' blood. Hummin' while he did it, too. Like it was just some chore. Just somethin' to do 'til the next thing."

"I'm sorry, I…"

She smiled and held up a hand, "I shot him in the asshole. Right between the cheeks. I shot guns before, but a target's different than a man, even an evil one. I hope it came out the front if you know what I mean. Next shot put him down, but I enjoyed that scream."

Henry showed both hands, "I'm not armed. I'm just like you, just gathering supplies for me and my little one."

He plucked a toy from the cart and showed it to her.

She nodded, a flicker of a smile passing over her face.

"It's good to see," she said, then tucked her knees to her chest and began to rise.

She had smoke in her voice and bunched lines around her lips. Her age was difficult to guess as the cigarettes had taken a toll on her skin, yellowish in color, the remnants of a summer tan that faded over the winter.

"I'm sorry about your husband. My, uh, wife…"

"Not your fault. Just like your wife wasn't mine. It was that bastard's fault and no one else."

"You may have saved my life. If you hadn't done what you needed to do, I could've been next."

She nodded, shoulders sagging as a long breath eased from her, thin, bird-like chest. As if forgetting she had the weapon, the woman frowned at it and secured it in the pouch of her hoodie.

"You should take it," she said, motioning toward the gun on the floor. "That was *his*. I won't touch it now. Not after what he used it for. Was gonna leave it there."

Henry swallowed the crabapple scaling his esophagus. The gun felt warm, as if its prior owner had only just dropped it.

"Know how to use it?" she asked.

"Yes," Henry said. "I've had to use them before."

She chewed her lip, eyes returning to the puddle of her husband's blood. Her jaw pulsed, eyebrows rippling as if she could not accept he was dead, that it was *his* blood on the floor.

"I haven't. Not like I did today," she said.

The words *I'm sorry* bubbled in Henry's throat, but she continued.

"He was in this aisle for me. Marcus was. Lookin' for Dr. Pepper 'cause it's my favorite. I know that in my heart. It's a strange world out there. Don't know if I belong in it anymore. Maybe I'll go to sleep tonight and that choice'll be taken from me. Where you headed?"

She extended a hand and Henry shook it.

"Henry."

"Jean."

"I hadn't figured out where to go from here. Had to get out of the city first. Was kind of making it up as I went along. How about you?"

"The plan was to find a place as far off the grid as possible. Whatever's goin' on in the city is gonna make its way to suburbs and towns we guessed. But they won't last forever, the Stargazers. They're not eatin'. Don't think they're meant to, you know? Some are dyin' in the streets from exposure, some gettin' attacked by dogs. Guess the real question is…what comes after them? Lots of homesteads in Texas. Lots of places to hide and wait it out."

"Self-sustaining?" Henry asked.

"That was the hope. Don't know about power, but I heard there's a sale on generators."

"Take one get one free!"

Jean patted her pouch as if to reassure herself the gun had not vanished and rapped a knuckle on the packaging of a plastic doll.

"What's her name?"

"Penny," Henry answered, realizing then his internal timer had faltered. "I-I should check on her. We're at the motel. The room with the SUV out front. Maybe we can talk strategy later? Would be good for her to see she's not alone."

"Sure," Jean said. "Gonna stock up on supplies. I, uh, would like some time with Marcus. He's in the back. I'll make my way over after."

"Looking forward to it. Feels awkward leaving now after you probably saved my life."

"Maybe you'll save mine and we'll call it even."

Henry smiled, leaned his weight on the shopping cart, and ushered it down the aisle. Maybe this would be the new normal. A daily contest for survival and the heroic efforts of strangers. A week ago, Henry ordered a book to prepare Penny for Pre-K. They read it every night and Penny dedicated much of her subsequent mornings to drawing the outfits she planned to wear to school. She laid a skirt and blouse combination across the foot of her bed despite the fact school was eight months away.

"You don't think you're going to want to wear it before then?" Henry asked.

"Daddy, it's for school!" Penny answered.

That future Penny, the one wearing a skirt and blouse and a sunflower headband would never exist. She would only ever be a projection in his mind, an unrealized destiny.

"Headin' out!" Henry called as he left the store.

"I'll be along this evenin'. Gotta surprise for the little one!"

The shopping cart rattled angrily over stray rocks in the parking lot. It felt like hours had passed, but he likely missed his goal by no more than five minutes.

"That's strange," Henry said, staring at the empty parking space where the truck had been.

"For my Mother"

2 February 2023, 7:47 PM User – **FeelthaBern38:**

I walked with my mother for hours, holding her hand as we followed the crowd through the city. I told her that I loved her, and then I told her why. "Love you" was something we said just before hanging up or right before I closed the door when leaving her place. Maybe it would have been strange to dedicate hours to telling her why, not practical in addition.

When this started, I made a plan with my mother, to call her every night at midnight. She would answer the phone and I would know she was safe, that she had not become one of them.

The plan endured for one night, because she did not answer the second time I called. I hoped she had fallen asleep, or that the phone malfunctioned. But her neighbor answered. That was our backup plan. She bundled up and walked through Mom's open front door.

No Mom.

I drove six hours to her retirement community, passed thousands of recently minted Stargazers all walking the same direction. Her footprints were visible in the soft, frosty grass. They continued down the sidewalk before fading into nothing. It wasn't difficult to track her. She was a few blocks from her duplex, pink robe fluttering in the wind like a superhero's cape.

The initial urge was to attempt to corral her, redirect her back toward her home. When I blocked her path, she walked around me. When I held her shoulders, she dug her heels in. Maybe a leash?

*It was during these efforts, to hold onto my mother, I began to share **why** she couldn't leave. From my first breath, she was there for me. She was exactly who I needed her to be at every stage of my life. She co-signed my love of books by giving me a ten-dollar check for the Scholastic Book Fair. That was ten dollars less she had for herself during a time we were struggling financially, and not once did she let me* know it. When school turned into a battlefield, she believed my sudden morning fevers, my forehead red from rubbing it in the hopes the friction would make it feel warm. The thermometer never corroborated my illness, so Mom said it must be broken.

When I introduced Mom to one male "friend" after another she never questioned it. I remember a phone conversation during which she told me about a male co-worker and his partner, how cute they were together and how she hoped someday the laws would change so they could marry. It was very obvious she was reading from a script. I could hear the pages flip as she did.

I told her how much it all meant. And the sun rose. The frost turned to dew then melted off the grass, transforming into a light mist before dissipating. I held her hand through it all. I poured into her the love she had shown me in so many ways. I understood I could not stop what was happening. The switch had been flipped. Maybe her essence was no longer tied to that body. It didn't really matter. I would have said those words to an empty room if necessary.

She had faults. She made mistakes. That was okay. I didn't need her to be perfect. I just needed her to be. And she was.

My mother's name would have graced no history books. After all of this is over, maybe the only thing left of her will be some junk mail turning to dust in a landfill. If I have learned anything from this experience, with my mother and within all of the chaos in the world, it is that love is a currency. When it is exchanged, though, both parties become richer. Someone smarter than me has probably said that in a more impactful way.

I let her go around lunchtime. I watched her pink, superhero cape shrink until it was no longer visible.

You are not your body, Mom. You are a passenger in my heart, forever.

2 February 2023, 8:10 PM User **– Ysewcirius!:**

Beautiful words for your mother. Well stated, OP.

2 February 2023, 8:12 PM User – **Danightstalka595:**

Hate to be "that" guy, but that's not what this forum is for. Maybe you could dress it up a bit? Have your mom get eaten alive by crows?

CHAPTER SIX – PROTECT

She slept through the sound of his entry, the crinkling of plastic as he prepared a late lunch for her. Henry knew he would eat to keep his energy up disregarding his appetite. But he could not purge the thought it could have been his blood on the tiles instead of Jean's husband. Penny would have lived the rest of her life never knowing why her father left.

Sandwich cut the way she preferred, chips arranged on a paper plate, he waited, watching her from a stiff armchair next to the circular table that looked like wood but felt like plastic.

Henry understood a nap simply rearranged the number of hours Penny would sleep, stealing them from the evening. That was okay. Schedules were quickly becoming a failed concept, as was the calendar.

Shit Henry thought *How do I explain Santa?*

Sometimes Judith responded to his internal questions. Hers was the voice of reason, often lacking nuance or kindness. She was not intentionally unkind in life. Kindness was a long and winding road to get to the same place as a blunt truth. The quickest path to any destination was a straight line. Though, occasionally straight lines passed directly through a minefield.

Henry would have almost a year to invent a new lore for Santa, and there was a better than good chance he would not live long enough to need it. He could become a

Stargazer that night. Or Penny could, and if that happened he had no reason to continue living.

There was a rumble from outside, one Henry guessed belonged to an old Ford truck. Maybe the owner had gone out for supplies as well. Penny roused, her hair a seaweed tangle obscuring her face.

"Daddy?"

"Just a second, sweetie," he said, darting to the door.

He glared through the peephole.

"Shit."

"Daddy…"

"Sorry. Potato."

"That's better."

The peephole was useless, and Henry stomped his foot at forgetting that fact. He parted the heavy curtain and the vertical blinds behind it.

"What in the…" he began. The truck was parked directly behind his SUV. There was no room to pull forward. The SUV was stuck.

"Daddy?" Penny said. Henry followed her pointing finger to the gun resting against his thigh.

"Oh! Don't worry about that."

"What's it for?"

He placed the gun on the table, hid his hands from view.

"Forgot I had it, sweetie. I ran across the street for food when you fell asleep. Got some other things for you," he said, pointing at the packages on the opposite bed, but Penny didn't take the bait. "There was an accident there before I got there. It's okay. I met a nice lady in the store and she's going to come by later."

Penny's eyes alternated between the gun and the toys, eventually settling on her father's face. He spoke with his scared voice, one that usually predicted a *shutdown*. That was her word for it, when her father only answered questions with grunts or head motions, when he stared at the floor as if it was the back of some house-sized monster and he had to keep his feet on it just so or risk waking it.

Penny placed two hands over her belly, the tang of sour cream and onion chips disrupting her thoughts. She found the lunch plate on the nightstand and forgot about everything else.

Henry was content to watch her chew, saying nothing. It was a small joy he imagined every parent felt, successfully feeding their finicky child. She wiped her gritty fingers on the comforter, spilled juice on the sheets.

"Daddy," Penny began, mouthful of sandwich. "Where do you think Mommy is?"

Henry crossed his legs, laid his hands in his lap. The truck parking behind the SUV was intentional. He felt it in his gut, in the extra blood flooding his muscles.

"Walking, probably. Something happened a few days ago, sweetie. No one understands what. People, lots of people—in fact just about everybody, started leaving their homes at night to stare at the sky."

"Did Mommy?"

He nodded, "Yes, last night. I fell asleep in your room and woke up early in the morning. Came downstairs to check on her and she was outside."

"Did you try to help?"

"There really isn't any *help* you can give them. *Stargazers* is what people call them. I made her as comfortable as possible. That was the best I could do."

The phone's ring was like a dagger in his ear canal. Penny screeched and burrowed into the pillow. Henry snatched the receiver.

"Who is this?"

"Good afternoon room one."

A man's voice, older than Henry by the sound of it, dripping with slime and bad intentions.

"Who are you? What is this?"

"Does my name really matter?"

"That your truck?"

"Ayuh. It is."

"Why'd you park behind me like that?"

"So, you wouldn't leave. Oh, and I did a little more than that if you want to take a look."

Henry walked around the bed and peeked through the window. His SUV was canted to the side, sinking on deflating tires. He lifted the gun from the table as Penny pressed herself deeper into the pillows.

"This is the hard part, room one. For you. Not for me. I'm taking the girl."

"Fuck you." Henry spat.

"And here's how it's gonna work. You're going to give her to me. Why? Because you won't have a choice."

"I'll kill you."

"You'll try. But, you know, there's no way out of these rooms except through that door you're probably staring at right now. Go ahead and open it and see if you don't catch a bullet in your ear. These cords stretch a long way, don't they? Come on out. You'll see me waving."

Henry considered opening the door and taking a shot. What if he missed?

"You're gonna give her to me in exactly five minutes. I'll give you that long to say goodbye. I *am* a monster, but you're giving me the gift of a lifetime of companionship. It's the least I can do. Now, before you start growling into the phone again about how you would never give her to me, I'll explain why that's not true.

"There is no way out of that room except that door, right? I know. I've stayed in this motel dozens of times over the years, including the room you're stayin' in. By the way, they never wash the sheets and I've been known to leave my mark, if you catch my drift. If your daughter has a rash on her pretty little face, well, won't be your problem much longer.

"If you don't give her to me five minutes after I hang up I'm gonna throw a brick through the window. Then I'm gonna follow that up with a gas can with a little, flamin' hankie stuffed inside. Then you'll either burn to death or run out with your clothes on fire. I'll try to put the flames out with my rifle. I'll even set it to *burst* for you.

"If you walk out alone, I'll shoot you. If you try to run I'll shoot you. I could shoot the dick off a fly with this thing I got in my hands. You won't make it two steps. And if you do, where you gonna go? You gonna run down the road with your girl in your arms hopin' I'm a good enough shot to kill you and not hit her?"

Penny watched her father pace. The gun was in his hand again.

"See, at the end of all of this we're gonna need to repopulate. Yeah, that's what you didn't wanna hear, huh? I understand. But it's true. This Stargazer shit is nuts, isn't it? Never had more fun in my life. You know what a Stargazer will do when you stick a knife in her? Nothing. Walk, and bleed. That's it. You can walk about a quarter mile with a knife in your kidneys, crawl another couple hundred feet. I've done a lot worse than that the last couple of days. Hard to pin someone down that keeps walking forward, but it's not so hard when they're legs are broken."

"I'll nev-"

"Buddy, I had the jump on you the moment you pulled in. Daughter still wearin' that nightgown? I watched you the whole time. Watched you leave her by herself. Could have taken her then but couldn't risk you gettin' me from behind. Been thinkin' about that gas can idea for years, just didn't have the can in the truck.

"Use your five minutes. Don't waste time comin' up with a plan to beat me. You ain't gonna survive this, but she might."

Silence.

Henry quietly padded over the carpet and placed the phone back in its cradle.

"Who was it, Daddy?" Penny asked, sheets pulled to her chin.

He never considered lying. The truth would be hard. There may be harder truths to come than this.

"A man staying in the motel. Remember that truck when we pulled in?"

She pulled the sheets higher, nodded.

"What did he say?" she asked, eyes locking onto the weapon against his thigh.

"He wants to hurt us."

She gasped, released the sheets and opened her arms. Henry perched her on his hip.

"It's okay, sweetie. I'm gonna do everything I can to keep you safe. This is one of those times I need you to do exactly what I say, yeah?"

She nodded.

"That means I need you to hide in the bathroom."

She shook her head, "Don't leave me!"

"I'm not. I'll be in this room. The bathroom is the safest place for you."

She shook her head again.

"Hey," he said. "You remember you asked why I love you?"

She nodded.

"It's not always the easiest thing to say, just because there is so *much* to say," he said, then took a long breath. "There were times in my life I didn't know why I kept going. Like when we go to the playground, and you run so much and so hard, you feel like you can't run anymore. It kind of felt like that, except I wasn't always running. Remember the story about the people shooting at me?"

She nodded.

"I was looking up at the stars and thinking how peaceful it must be up there. I was in a lot of pain after things settled, in my body and up here," Henry said, tapping his head. "Each time I closed my eyes it felt like going home. Like I belonged there. It's that feeling you get after the books are read and we're just lying in the darkness waiting for sleep to come. But there was something else. It's something I felt then, and I think I felt it all my life. It was something pulling on me, pulling on that part of me that's not my body or my mind."

She arched her eyebrows, fingers rubbing the stubble of his chin.

"It was you," he said.

"Me?"

"I think so. Before you had a name. Before you had a body. You were just this little tug in my chest. Every time I closed my eyes and it felt so peaceful…"

She mimed plucking something from his chest.

He chuckled, "Not that hard, but yes. It was like that. Anytime I thought the stars were home I felt it. Felt you. I knew that home was wherever you were.

"Now, I need you to wait in the bathroom. I'm going to turn the water on so you can't hear as well. Daddy might have to say some words you don't like, and that man won't understand about potato."

"Okay, Daddy," Penny said, squeezing his neck until he made fake choking sounds.

"Don't come out until I knock. Okay? It's gonna get loud. I'm gonna to have to shoot the gun, but it's for show, okay? Don't make a single sound. No matter how much you want to. No matter what you hear. Don't make a sound."

"Okay, Daddy."

She sat on the mat in front of the sink, and he brought her books. She selected the one with the tiger in the red sweater. It was about being brave. She read aloud the pages she knew by heart as Henry stood in the doorway. He would not prepare her for the possibility of him not coming back.

***

"Five minutes is up. Send her out."

"Sure thing. Come and take her from me."

"That really the way you want this to go, buddy? You want your daughter to turn into a charcoal briquette?"

"There's hot dogs across the street. Store brand stuff but they'll do. Grab some marshmallows while you're at it."

"You dumb sonofabitch. I was gonna take it easy on her. Let her wait 'til she got some grass on the field. Maybe not now. She's gonna grow up hatin' you, know that? When she's cryin' under me I'll tell her *you* gave her up."

"No. You won't," Henry said, then held the phone away from him and aimed the gun at the pillows. "I'm sorry, sweetie."

The phone slipped from his grasp.

"Wait! Don't d-"
POW
POW

Thirty seconds later, a brick flew through the window. Another brick followed, both cartwheeling off the mattress. A rifle muzzle probed the frame, clearing shark teeth glass.

"You dumb sonofabitch..." the man muttered, then laid a towel over the bottom of the frame. The muzzle batted aside the vertical blinds and stabbed at the curtain. A heavy, black boot passed over the threshold, crunching glass into the carpet. A second boot joined it. He waited, head cocked to the side, listening to the sound of running water in the bathroom. Looking straight forward, just the tip of his nose was visible protruding from within the curtains.

Henry exhaled.
"Wha-"
POW
POW
POW
POW

Henry never saw his face. The man pivoted toward the parking lot and slumped as if his spinal cord was severed, taking the curtains down with him. Sunlight flooded the room. His final breath was a wheeze choked with blood.

"I'm okay! Stay in there, Penny! I'm okay!"

Henry tossed the bricks outside, then threw the comforter over the man, then turned as the sound of rushing water grew louder.

"It's me. I'm okay, sweetie," Henry said, breathless.

The door closed.

Henry sat on the edge of the bed, watched sunlight flare through chunks of broken glass, painting small rainbows on the floor. How many times would he have to do this? It felt like death was a satellite growing closer and closer with each orbit.

The crunch of gravel under tires wrenched him out of his daydream. He had three bullets left. Fuck, what if the dead man had friends?

Henry duckwalked next to him, the carpet squelching as he adjusted his position. The adrenaline settling into his muscles made his veins feel heavy, made the gun feel like a forty-pound dumbbell. His trigger finger shook.

A vehicle door slammed. Slow steps followed. Maybe they would just move on. See the dead man falling out of the window and decide against exploring further.

Crunch

Crunch

Crunch

"My God," a whisper.

Henry pursed his lips, tried to make his breaths silent.

"Penny?" a smoky voice called.

"Jean?" Henry answered.

"Jesus Christ, Henry! Are you in there?"

They stood, looking at each other. The little black and white dog in her arms thrashed to get to Henry, whining like a piglet.

"It was my fault," Henry said.

"No. Henry, it was not your fault. Just like Marcus wasn't my fault. It was *his* fault. Whatever he did or was gonna do he deserved it."

"How do you know? We just met."

She winked, gum-coated tongue darting for a second. She blew a bubble and popped it.

"I can tell. You can't hide evil. It's in the eyes," she said, then stood on tiptoe and peered over his shoulder. "Why hello! Are you Penny? This is Misfit. I call her that because she's a misfit. We used to call her Domino, but it didn't fit. Would you like to meet her?"

***

They moved to the opposite side of the motel, facing away from the street. Penny chased Misfit with a feather she found in the parking lot. Jean propped a chair beneath the doorframe and watched, eyes misting as the little girl and little dog ran figure eights around the room.

"You hungry?" Henry asked late in the afternoon. "I don't think I've eaten for a day or so. Had so much adrenaline in my body kinda felt sick from it."

Jean winked. Henry could tell that was going to be her thing.

"I'll take care of dinner. Keep an eye on Misfit."

Henry collapsed onto the bed. Within a few minutes he detected an unmistakable scent, one popular in his neighborhood on warm holidays. With a backdrop of yips and squeals, he slipped easily into sleep.

***

"Daddy! Daddy, it's dinnertime!"

Penny's heart-shaped face beamed in the doorway, milky evening light behind her. Henry clawed for purchase, pulling himself to a seated position. He felt hungover.

"Sorry," Henry muttered, exiting the room and finding Jean and Penny seated around a small, plastic table.

"You needed it. Can't drive on empty," Jean said with a wink.

It was the best burger he'd ever tasted. The stars pinned darkness to the sky, the moon hiding somewhere beyond their sight. Penny peppered Jean with questions, mostly about Misfit, until her letters grew as soft as warm dough. Misfit fell asleep on her lap, and they alternated snores as Jean and Henry made plans to leave together the following morning.

"...out near Marfa. That's a long drive from here, but it's elevated. Temperature's not what you'd expect for the des-"

Henry held up a finger, turned his face to the side.

"Do you hear that?" he asked a moment later

The dying embers of the portable grill lent a soft glow to her face. She cupped a hand around her ear and frowned.

"Hearin's not so good. Marcus got into motorcycles after he retired. Loud ones. Kind of sounds like..." she trailed off.

"Like the wind through the trees, but not quite."

Henry stood, bent to retrieve his weapon. He looked to Jean then to Penny.

"Go on."

The crunch of rocks eliminated any chance of moving undetected. In between the steps, the sound grew sharper edges. Not quite wind but something like distant rain. Henry turned a corner, gun held in front of him.

"Oh...wow."

The weapon lowered of its own accord.

"Jean!" he whisper-shouted.

Misfit roused but did not follow her owner as she joined Henry.

They watched in silence as the river of humanity passed. It stretched forever into darkness.

"Well, they caught up to us," Jean said.

"Hell of a walk from the city."

"Drive was bad enough."

"Wonder where they're going."

Jean sighed, "That's the million-dollar question, isn't it? Where they're goin', what they're doin'. Find that out and we might figure out why. Why did this happen?"

Henry walked forward a few paces. The lights in the supermarket parking lot did not quite reach the road, and the motel's light was hardly better than a candle's glow.

"What is it? Lookin' for someone?" Jean asked.

He hadn't been looking for Judith, could not have distinguished her from the tide of billowing nightgowns. Something else caught his eye.

"What is it, Henry?" Jean asked, concern slipping into her voice.

"I- I don't know. I think—are they looking at us?"

"I Found a Rogue Stargazer"

3 February 2023, 4:38 PM, User – **Colorado_Kid14:**

Guess I couldn't stay away. Can you blame me? I found my cabin in the woods. Beautiful place. Remote. I was okay not having creature comforts, you know? Whoever owned it stocked it well enough, if you don't mind canned everything.

There's a generator, which is nice. The snow's up to my knees right now, gets to single digits at night. But just a couple days in I had to start rationing fuel. That was one thing not stocked in abundance. Guess the owner (hunter-type if the dead animals mounted to the wall are any indication) brought that with him when he visited the cabin.

I could probably have rationed better. Could have lasted ten days, maybe two weeks wearing layers at all times. The cabin was not a home, just a pit stop along the way to wherever home was. I'm thinking Utah, maybe. Does Utah have any lakes without salt in them? Water's probably going to be an issue.

Anyway. Getting off track. I am writing this from a house north and west of Pueblo. Dial-up still works, but not sure for how long. I'll make my way back to the cabin but wanted to share this information. The title is not clickbait, though like most posts in this forum prior to the end of the world I don't have a concrete explanation, just guesses.

Luckily, the knee-high snow is old snow and the path to civilization was mostly clear. I passed a few farms before I reached the county road leading me to the first town. There were no people, not that I expected any, but the town had not been demolished. I'm sure that will come eventually.

I loaded up with fuel and produce. Don't imagine I'll have access to avocados in the near future, so I loaded up on them. Never got one of those suckers to grow before, but I think I'll have time to really dedicate myself to it now. Do they grow avocados in Utah? Seems like a California thing.

Honestly, I was wasting time. Despite my personal belief I could live in isolation for as long as was needed, I missed people. Although they were gone, I was surrounded by the evidence of the lives they led. "Missing cat" posters taped to store windows, bicycles chained to racks, an old banner arching over Main Street for last year's "Holiday Lights" parade. It was both peaceful and heartbreaking.

The temperature dropped during my brief sojourn through town, and the wind picked up, turning tree branches into snake rattles. It was an hour to the cabin in good weather. I retraced my path out of town, then saw something that made me stop.

There was a Stargazer in the middle of the road. I will caveat that is an assumption, not a provable fact. However, he was wearing the unofficial uniform, plaid pajamas and an over-sized t-shirt. I had never seen a Stargazer not actively gazing, walking, or performing some other task. (I have my suspicions about what they're doing, but will add those to the end of this post.) It was mostly a "huh?" moment and I accelerated, intending to drive around the man.

He looked up, made eye contact with me, and began a full sprint towards my vehicle. I have never seen a human being run like that. He brandished a weapon of some sort. I guess I mentally blocked it out during my first analysis. I was so accustomed to seeing Stargazers a certain way I didn't notice the tire iron, or whatever it was.

His intent was to kill me. I have no doubts about that. His face did not change. It still had that placid, Stargazer look to it. I reversed, but he was making up ground. Put it in drive and gunned it. The tire iron hit the windshield with a glancing blow, cracking the glass but not penetrating it. The impact knocked him to the ground, but by the time I checked my rearview he was already up and running at me.

I passed two bodies in the street the first block, maybe more. Honestly, I was mostly looking at the rearview. I didn't think about them in the moment. There were Stargazer bodies here and there, those that succumbed to the elements. In the same way I blocked out his weapon I blocked out their attire. They were dressed for winter, which means they weren't Stargazers.

Snow began to fall, and I don't have chains for these tires. I found an abandoned house not far from the road that would lead me back to the cabin. That's where I am right now. I unloaded what I needed while I wait for the weather to pass, still a bit shaky from the encounter. I guess that's why I didn't notice the blood on the windshield. Blood from the tire iron. Blood from the people in the street.

There are a few possibilities, but the only one that makes sense is it was a rogue Stargazer. (See, told you it wasn't clickbait) If it was a non-Stargazer he would have been dressed for the weather. I tried to convince myself he was just a crazy person. Maybe they let psych patients out like they did with some of the prisoners. The logic makes sense, but I come back to the running, to the face. He ran as though he learned it from an instruction manual if you can picture that.

What does it mean? Maybe just a one-off. Obviously, whatever is happening to them starts upstairs (points to head). Even the best surgeon's going to nick an artery every once in a career. Start messing with the gray matter and there's bound to be a few screw ups. I don't think that's the case, though. I wish it was. It would be less to worry about.

I'm dancing around the words I want to say because I really want to be wrong.

For whatever reason, **we** are not Stargazers. Maybe we'll transition tonight, who knows. But if the plan was for **everyone** to become a Stargazer...we slipped through the cracks. If that is the case, then the man from Main Street might be an **adjustment** to the plan. A correction. Each of them has had a purpose. Some to destroy, some to build, some simply to die if the reports are true. I think this is a new purpose. To destroy those of us who remain, who have not been turned. From a big picture perspective, it's kind of like moving into a new house. Change the things you don't like about it before you move in, spray for pests. The homeowner doesn't do those things. Someone else does. And once the task is done, you don't have a need for an exterminator, right? You don't expect them to fix your shingles. I'm thinking about the sailors from the first days of this nightmare. They scuttled (I think that's the right word for *it) the ship and then...you know what happened. No need for them after the task was done.*

I'm going to keep dancing around that last thought. I'm not ready to commit to it.

Don't trust a Stargazer. I'm not.

3 February 2023, 5:25 PM User – **OfficialNoSleep:**

Taco Bell!!

3 February 2023, 5:32 PM User – **OfficialNoSleep:**

Is this thing on? We not doing that joke anymore?

CHAPTER SEVEN – SUNRISE

Henry wrestled with the sheets twisted around his arms as the phone's chime set fire to his dreams. Penny groaned and sandwiched her head between two pillows. The ring was loud enough to disturb Misfit in the neighboring room.

"Hello?"

"Sorry to wake you. It's Jean," she said, then chuckled. "Not like you were expectin' anyone else."

"What's up?"

"Last night, the Stargazers, you thought one was lookin' at you at first."

"Yeah, until all of them stopped and looked at the sky. I guess that one was a few seconds early."

"Maybe. Might have nothin' to do with what I'm lookin' at now."

Henry swiveled his legs over the edge of the bed, planted his feet on the carpet and grimaced.

"What are you looking at now?"

He heard the sound of blinds clacking against one another.

"There's a couple of 'em outside. Starin' at our doors."

"What?"

Henry cringed as the carpet caressed the soles of his feet. He pulled the curtain aside and peeked through a gap in the blinds.

"No shit…" he muttered.

"Daddy!" Penny moaned, voice muffled by the pillow.

"I know, right? I was about to let Misfit out to do her business but thought to check first. You know, 'cause of the incidents yesterday. I can't see the rest of 'em from here. The group from last night. I imagine they started walkin' again when the sun came up. Seems to be their way."

"You said there's two?"

"Yeah, one's kinda wanderin'. She's got a pipe or somethin' in her hand."

"A pipe?"

"Yeah. The one you can see has somethin' too. It's behind him some. Can't really make it out."

To Henry it was just a black shadow to the right of the Stargazer's pajama pants.

"So what do we do?"

Jean's laugh turned ragged in her chest, ended with a brief coughing fit.

"Excuse me. Sorry. I was gonna ask you the same thing. I guess we could wait 'em out. It's not like we don't have the time for it. I don't really mind if Misfit makes a mess in here. Be leavin' soon enough and I don't think they're gonna charge me for it."

Henry allowed the blinds to fall back into place. He pivoted to find Penny sitting on the bed with her arms folded, hair a rat's nest he preemptively regretted having to brush out.

"We have food and water. I guess if they don't start tearing the town apart we'd be okay. Depending on when they…turned they might not last too long, physically. But what makes you think they're targeting us?"

"A gut feelin', mostly. A bit of logic too, I guess. I seen 'em in the city with tools, drivin' a forklift even. Always a purpose to it. They didn't just pick up a hammer for sentimental reasons. So, if they're not destroyin' the motel they must have some other purpose. Since they're lingerin' around our rooms I would guess that purpose is us."

"Why not just come at us now?"

"Don't know. Guess we can ask, huh?"

"I got his rifle. The guy from yesterday. It would be two easy shots for me, but it feels different. *He* was coming after us. It was defensive. I don't know if I can start killing people, Stargazers or not, because of something they *might* do."

"Yeah."

"What if they all snap out of it ten minutes from now?"

"Not likely."

"I know it's not. But what happened to them was unlikely as well."

"So...wait?"

Henry sighed, "I guess. We have enough to get by for a few days if it takes that long."

"I'll be next door. Gonna turn that awful ringer off, though. Just knock on the wall and I'll answer the phone right after if you need to call me."

"I'll do the same."

He hung up under Penny's watchful gaze.

"What?"

"I wanna see Misfit."

"You'll get to, sweetie. Just playing it safe for now."

"Safe from what?"

"You know all those people we passed? The ones from the neighborhood and on the side of the road while we were driving out of the city?"

"Yeah."

"They haven't paid attention to us before, but there's a couple of 'em outside and Jean thinks, I guess I do too, that they're waiting for us to come out."

"Why?"

"Probably not good reasons. Jean and I decided we're going to keep to the rooms for now. Maybe they'll move on after tonight."

"So, we're stuck inside? No Misfit?"

Henry sat beside her on the bed, reached a hand for a tangle of hair, which she shied away from.

"For now. Think of it like camping."

Penny didn't buy it.

"We don't have marshmallows."

"I'll make up for it. We'll have a fire and everything."

***

Time passed quicker than he would have guessed. They read books and played games, built forts with the scant furniture in the room. Henry called Jean around lunchtime and let Penny bark into the phone to let Misfit know she had not abandoned her. Without refrigeration, Henry was forced to flush the perishable food down the toilet, but Penny was more than happy to eat sour cream and onion chips and apples.

During lulls in their games, Penny asked about her mother, where she might be.

"Hopefully somewhere beautiful, maybe where we used to hike?" Henry offered.

"Maybe," Penny said, suddenly becoming fascinated with her fingers.

They napped through the afternoon and roused to the sound of thunder.

"I saw the other one, the rover you mentioned. Walked by a few minutes ago, seems to be doing laps around the motel, but it was too dark for a good look," Henry said.

"I guess if we time it right we only need to worry about the one."

"Time it?"

"If we need to leave. Maybe it was only cities gettin' torn down. If not, they'll be here sooner than later."

"But why didn't the group last night..." Henry began.

"Henry, you're askin' questions can't be answered. I think *maybe* is gonna be our word of the day from now on. Maybe they're tearin' down the next town on the map. Maybe they're at the end of their usefulness and they're gonna jump in a lake or walk off a cliff."

"You're right. Good to have a plan even if we're operating in the dark."

The drumbeat of rain accelerated from a whisper to a dull roar.

"Look, you've got the newer ride. If we have to make a run for it, I'd trust your wheels over mine."

"Actually, the wheels are the part I don't trust. The guy from yesterday slashed 'em."

"That right? Well, guess it's Ol' Reliable then. And, Henry, if it comes down to having to shoot 'em I hope you can do what's needed."

Henry rubbed the scars on his chest, predicting an itch that failed to develop.

"If it comes down to it. I think the walls are thin enough we can just shout something. *Time to go!* Something like that. We both make a break for Ol' Reliable. Leave everything behind. If we get separated, just do what's best for ourselves. We'll keep traveling west, look for one of those homesteads you mentioned."

"If we get separated try to lead me back to you. Now, let me say good night to that sweet kiddo."

Penny took the phone and issued a stream of consciousness series of thoughts that persisted, uninterrupted, for half an hour.

"Jean? Jean?" Penny said, hearing only silence. "I think she fell asleep."

Henry put a hand over his mouth as if holding back laughter and took the phone.

***

Penny's eyes ricocheted around the room, often landing on the television, confusion and sadness at war on her face. She missed the songs and music mostly. They were a reason to get off the couch and dance around, take her father's hands and pull him away from whatever had his attention. That outlet was gone, and the games were making her tired. More than anything, she wanted to be in her own bed. It was smaller, but it was hers. There were so many questions she did not know how to ask. Questions she knew might cause her father to rub his hands together and stare at the floor. She wanted to know when they were going back home, when she could see her friend across the street again. Testing the waters of that question, though, sent her father pacing around the room.

There was something outside. She understood that from the conversations between her father and Jean. They were people, but the word he used was different. Penny watched her father part the blinds at least once every half hour, but when she attempted it, he barked at her to get away from the window.

They fell asleep independently and unplanned, her father with a book on his chest and her with a plastic harmonica in her hand. Rain pelted the roof, but the thunder never rose above a rumble.

***

A dream within a dream, of waking to find Judith beside him. It was their room, not the motel. With the watery logic of dreams, though, this realization faded like smoke from a dying ember.

"Where were you?" he asked, snaking an arm around her midsection.

He followed the question with a gentle squeeze, believing her to still be asleep.

"Babe?"

He planted a kiss on the nape of her neck, probed the cool terrain of the bed until he found her fingers. She usually placed a pillow between them, for her lower back, she said. The absence of a pillow must have been an invitation then.

"Babe?"

Henry gave her a little nudge, squeezed her hand in concert. He propped himself on his elbows, hovered above her searching for an indication of consciousness. Her mouth was open as if frozen just before gasping for breath. He waved a hand in front of her unblinking eyes.

"Judith?"

"Mommy?" she said though her lips did not move.

"Babe, what?"

"Mommy!"

Judith's hand smacked the nightstand, shoved the lamp onto the floor. It thumped but did not shatter, the action and its corresponding sound off by several seconds.

Henry blinked half a dozen times, the dream with its claws sunk into his reality.

"Judith?" he mumbled.

The scent of sour cream and onion chips and the cold stiffness of the motel sheets wrenched the dream claws from his mind. No, it was Penny, not Judith. Penny standing in front of the window staring up at...

The pipe burst through the glass at the same moment Henry thrashed free of the sheets, landing one hand on Penny's shoulder. Judith punched an arm through the ragged hole in the window, glass carving her forearm to bloody ribbons. Her fingers snagged the frilly sleeve of Penny's nightgown.

Her jacket was gone, the clothes beneath it pasted wetly to her body. The blood coursing from her arm soaked into Penny's nightgown, lubricating her fingers so that the fabric slipped free. Penny mashed herself into her father's chest as the red, glistening arm retracted through the hole in the glass.

She was a haggard thing, backlit by lightning barricaded within the storm. How far was it from the city? Fifty or sixty miles? She walked that distance without a morsel of food, without considering turning her head to the sky to drink. She was at the limit of what her body could endure before the architecture crumbled. But there was only this task before her, this task and then a great black emptiness.

"Oh, shit. Oh, fuck," Henry whispered.

He forgot the words he was supposed to say to alert Jean. Penny did not hear or did not care about his breech of decorum. She shed the nightgown like a discarded snakeskin, her mother's blood streaking her left arm as Judith reared back again, pipe in hand.

There were two guns within feet of him. This could be over. Penny would not understand, not then and maybe not for years if ever. The pipe, about the diameter of a quarter and the length of Judith's arm, doubled the size of the hole, glass drizzling over the carpet.

"Jean!" Henry yelled. "I- we need help!"

Penny unleashed the scream building pressure in her chest, flattened herself against the opposite wall.

"Wha?" Jean called from the neighboring room as Misfit's rapid-fire bark joined the rising crescendo.

"Fuck! We need help! The other Star-" Henry began, words interrupted by a third blow to the window. "It's my wife out there!"

Henry seized the handgun and joined Penny across the room. The blows came quicker now. With his left hand, Henry caressed the back of Penny's head. With his right he aimed a gun at the bleeding specter of his wife. There was only one decision. His mind understood it, but not his finger. Just a flicker and it would end, one quick squeeze would send the woman who sometimes failed at loving him, but loved him nonetheless, reeling backwards into the parking lot. There the rain would purify her wounds, dilute the blood until it was a hint of pink amid the puddles.

He couldn't do it.

She cleared enough glass to step halfway into the room.

"Daddy she's coming!" Penny squealed.

With each second that passed his options dwindled until there would be only one. To make a break for the door would put Penny within arm's reach. They could hide in the bathroom but there was no lock on the door.

Judith stood on the rubble, one barefoot bleeding, the other safely within its boot. Her eyes fixed on Penny without malice or venom. She adjusted her grip on the pipe and took a step forward.

One little squeeze, maybe just enough to put her on the floor. Would Penny appreciate the difference? That he had not killed her mother but bought them time to escape? His trigger finger disconnected from his mind. He no longer had control. Henry put himself between his daughter and his wife, ready to take the first blow and unable to do what was necessary to prevent it from coming.

"Henry!"

Judith careened to the side, and Jean appeared behind her.

"Just go! I'll catch up!"

Judith was already on her feet.

"Go!"

There was a gun in Jean's hand, not aimed at Judith for the moment.

"Go!"

Henry scooped Penny into his arms and dashed out the door into the storm. Ol' Reliable was running, the windows foggy and a small, black and white dog with its nose pressed to the glass. The dog tumbled into Penny's arms as the door opened.

"Go Henry!" Jean screamed, her thin, wiry arms coiled around Judith.

Henry slammed the door, threw Ol' Reliable into reverse, and sprayed gravel across the parking lot as he roared into darkness with the sun rising behind.

This time, he did not look back.

"The Morning Never Came"

3 February 2023, 9:09 AM User – **SunEater_10:**

Does it feel that way to you? You went to sleep one night and drifted from dream to dream to dream. Maybe we are still in our beds. Maybe it is only me. Is this what death feels like? Are my children holding vigil by my bed as my body fights a disease my dreams hide from me?

I searched the stars for answers last night, in my dream or this awful new reality. The answer must be there, right? If not an answer then a clue. But I saw only stars.

Dogs roam the streets trailing leashes, tags advertising homes that no longer exist. Soon, they will forget their names. They will forget their families. So will the rest of the world. In a thousand years humanity might only exist in radio waves traveling the cosmos, voices of the long dead whose descendants died with open mouths, unable to scream.

I hope it is only my dreams. I hope I slip quietly into that darkness between stars.

CHAPTER EIGHT – LIGHTS

"Daddy, that's a lot!" Penny said.

"It's the Fourth of July!" Henry replied, dumping the fireworks on the sun-parched earth.

"What's that mean?"

Henry dusted his hands on his jeans, "Well, we've gotta send up the flares for Jean like normal. Five o'clock on the dot. Then when it gets dark we'll light these. It's something we used to do before."

"Why?"

Misfit kicked her little legs until Penny released her to roam the stubble.

"Just one of those things. Like hanging up a stocking for Santa, right? Hiding eggs on Easter? On the Fourth of July you blow stuff up. You fell asleep before the fireworks started last year. Don't know how they didn't wake you up."

"Do you think she's out there?"

Henry flashed back to the morning at the motel. His last glimpse of Jean was a blur of color seen through sheets of rain. Judith strained within Jean's clutches, mannequin face detached from the rest of her body. He drove until the sun chased the clouds away. Turn around or keep going? He debated the merits but kept going, sparse trees relinquishing the landscape to desert.

They slept in the parking lot of a gas station, put hundreds of miles beneath the tires of Ol' Reliable searching for a house that could become a home. After a handful of false leads, they found it north and east of the town of Alpine. In the shadow of a mesa, hidden from the highway, the compound had a previous life as an eco-tourist destination. Henry freed the skittish horses they encountered, their backs scooped from years of trail rides. Some took off as if their hooves were on fire. Two stayed behind.

There was a spring, a vegetable garden, peach trees, and canned goods to feed them for years to come. The only thing missing was Jean, but Henry had hope. They drove back a few weeks after the morning attack and found the town leveled, the grocery store and motel both indistinguishable from their parking lots. They met no Stargazers, but there was evidence they were not alone.

A gas station off the highway had been broken into, the cigarettes and Dr. Pepper ransacked. Jean promised to quit smoking *eventually*, she'd said. A sticky note with a smiley face drawn on it was pasted to a bag of sour cream and onion chips. Beneath it was the wrinkled picture of Penny he had placed in Judith's pocket. He left a note for her. Not his address as he did not know who else might read it. Just enough to get her looking in the sky at the right time of day. Henry believed she was out there, roaming tens of thousands of square miles of Texas desert. He believed she would see the flare one day. He owed it to Misfit to keep trying.

"Yes, but it's kind of like a big, big, big game of hide and seek. Do you see those mountains?" Henry said, pointing.

Penny nodded.

"I guess we don't have countries anymore, but those used to be in Mexico. Can you believe that? You can see another country from here!"

Penny nodded, then took off after Misfit.

At exactly five o'clock, according to his watch, they sent a flare into the sky. After the sun dipped behind the western mountains and the orange bled from the sky, Henry fired off the first volley of fireworks. The noise sent Misfit sprinting into the night, and the celebration transitioned to a backyard fire, where Penny chucked blackened marshmallows into the grass, her tongue a peeking worm.

"Do you think we'll see the elephants again?" Penny asked.

"I don't know, sweetie. That was cool, though, huh?"

"Wonder where they went…"

"Well, they can go anywhere. They're elephants! That's funny to think about, though. There may be more elephants in Texas than people."

After having her fill of marshmallows, she crawled, sticky-fingered and sleepy-eyed into his lap. She listened to her father talk about the stars as her eyelids fluttered.

"Hey," Penny said, little finger limply aimed at a cluster of stars. "That's us. You, me, and Misfit."

***

He woke sometime after midnight. Misfit was in her usual place beside him, but Penny was not on the other side of her.

"Penny?"

He sat up, eyes adjusting to the darkness. Penny rarely needed the bathroom at night, but he eased out of bed to check.

No Penny.

He called her name loud enough to wake Misfit, who followed him as he searched the home. Sweat dotted his brow and he scratched his chest, running out of rooms to explore.

He saw her through the window. She was a little pale stripe on the lawn, head tilted to the sky.

Henry felt that strange, familiar numbness in his extremities. He felt the gravity of her, little ghost hands tugging at the core of him, that weightless mass that grounded him within his body. He staggered on wooden legs across the lawn, collapsing behind her.

No he thought, the only word his mind could offer, repeated on a loop. *No, no, no, no…*

"Penny…" he whispered.

She turned to find her father's face hidden behind his fingers.

Confused, she grasped his chin and directed his gaze.

"Daddy look. Look at all the pretty lights."

"I Was a Failed Stargazer"

1 February 2023, 2:17 PM User – **3kidsinatrenchcoat:**

I don't have clear memories of the moment I woke and left my bedroom to stand, barefoot in the snow, gazing at a night sky of stars and shredded clouds. It was like being on autopilot, like when your mind goes wandering during the drive home from work. I was a passenger in my body, aware of my movements but unable to alter them, aware of needles in my feet and cold fire in my ears.

Pictures infiltrated my mind, instructions I imagine, too fast for me to understand them, to commit anything to memory. At some level below my conscious thought my mind understood. The information was not taught to me. I did not learn it. It was stored in my brain, a place I could not access but I could sense the borders of.

I lost feeling in my feet and snot trickled into my open mouth. The "me" real estate in my brain shrunk as the borders damming this new information grew.

It was agony.

I was circling a drain, my destination not darkness but nothingness. Pain followed me down the drain until it was the only thing I understood. This persisted for hours, the blackened sky graying as light crept over the horizon.

Then it stopped, as if in the middle of a download the electricity went out.

I climbed out of the drain, moored myself within this aching body with blisters on my toes and fingers. By simply existing I reclaim the mental territory I lost.

*The information I was sent is still within me. The dam is cracking, and I can see the images now, can see what I was meant to do. It is one small slice of what **we** were meant to do.*

Prepare.

Run if you want. Hide if you want. If you are meant to become a Stargazer there is nowhere you can run or hide that will prevent it from happening.

They are coming.

ACKNOWLEDGMENTS

This story is dedicated to my daughter, Magnolia AKA Maggie. Penny is named after the character in a book I used to read to Maggie titled *A Dollar for Penny*. It was one of the first non-baby books she enjoyed. I have fond memories of reading that book to her while living on Guam.

Misfit, though not thoroughly described, represents our Japanese Chin, Abbie, who is also a misfit.

The story utilizes forum postings reminiscent of Reddit's NoSleep. As a writer, I only posted a couple of stories there, however I have been fortunate to have many stories adapted by *The NoSleep Podcast*. I used the forum posts to fill in the gaps of what Henry could not know or understand. I also had fun with the usernames as there was not a lot of room for humor in the main story.

I wrote, on average, 1000 words a day for about twenty-eight straight days to complete this novella. The bones around which the novella was crafted was a short story I had not written, but intended to, as somewhat of a gag. That story was called "Agape" and featured the same phenomenon of people staring at the sky, though during daytime and it was everyone at the same time except for the main character. I'll keep the gag private for now in case I ever write it. I held onto the imagery even as I avoided writing the story to work on other projects. The shift from day to night was the catalyst for the formation of the rest of *Stargazers* in my mind.

Although I am a military member and have deployed, I have never been in danger in the way Henry has. I also did not want what haunts him to come across as exploitative. I have met many servicemen and women impacted by combat. I thought of them while writing, but only hinted at what he might have endured out of respect for their experiences as they are not my own.

The post "The Morning Never Came" by user SunEater_10 is a shoutout to the band Swallow the Sun. Their album, *The Morning Never Came*, was in constant rotation on my playlist while writing.

Finally, these are the bands I listened to while writing this novella: Swallow the Sun, Knocked Loose, Jinjer, Draconian, Spiritbox, Rivers of Nihil, Fires in the Distance, Katatonia, and Insomnium among others.

LP Hernandez is an author of horror and speculative fiction. His stories have been featured in anthologies from Dark Matter Magazine, Cemetery Gates Media, and Sinister Smile Press among others. He is a regular contributor to *The NoSleep Podcast* and was privileged to helm the Season 16 finale. He has released two short story collections including the fully illustrated *The Rat King*. When not writing, LP serves as a medical administrator in the U.S. Air Force. He is a husband, father, and a dedicated metalhead. *Stargazers* is his first novella.

You can find links to LP's work at his website:
www.lphernandez.com

He is most active on Twitter:
www.twitter.com/thelphernandez

But does maintain a Facebook page:
www.facebook.com/authorlphernandez

Printed in Great Britain
by Amazon